THE BODY ELECTROCUTION

BOBBI SUE BAXTER MYSTERIES BOOK 2

Marissa Shrock

CIMELIAPRESS

The Body Electrocution

© 2023 by Marissa Shrock

All rights reserved.

Published by Cimelia Press, Greentown, Indiana

Printed in the United States of America

Print ISBN-13: 978-0-9969879-9-8

Library of Congress Control Number: 2023904799

CHAPTER 1

JUNE 1988

"Don't look now, Bobbi Sue, but Hemi Miller and his fiancée just walked in." Misty Ambrose perched on her usual barstool next to mine at Tate's Place.

"You say that like he's a big deal." Staring straight ahead, I swirled the ice in my glass and tapped my foot along with Def Leppard while "Pour Some Sugar on Me" played on the juke box.

"You have feelings for him, so don't even try to tell me he isn't," she whispered and tossed her curly red hair over her shoulder.

"He isn't."

"I don't believe you."

"Suit yourself."

My life had been hectic lately, and I could've used a quiet night at home reading. Instead, Misty had convinced me to join her at the local bar, which was the most exciting place to be on a Friday night in our hometown.

That wasn't saying much.

She stuck out her lip and glanced toward Hemi and Leslie. "She's not as pretty as you," she whispered.

"Get real." I emitted a wry laugh. "You're carrying the supportive friend act a little too far, don't you think?"

1

Leslie's feathery blond hair and innocent looking brown eyes were a much more compelling combination than my blue-gray eyes and shoulder-length brown hair. I was attractive and skinny enough, though my ears were too big for my liking, but it was fair to say I wouldn't be entering next year's Soybean Queen Pageant.

For so many reasons.

"She looks like an airhead," Misty said. "And before you can say it, I know. It takes one to know one."

Misty loved playing the role of bimbette—but I knew better than to buy it. "Wasn't going to." I drained my Coke.

"But you were thinking it."

"Actually, I was thinking I should've stayed home and read a book." I slammed my glass against the bar. "Kurt, may I please have a refill?"

Kurt Conway had a smile that made most women forget his short stature, including Misty, who frequently used the lame excuse that she was keeping Kurt company while he worked.

He glanced at Misty in her short denim skirt and swiped up my glass. "Sure you don't want something stronger?"

"No thank you."

"She's pretending she doesn't care about Hemi Miller." Misty sipped her beer.

"I don't need to pretend. He's off the market, we're just friends, and I was never looking in the first place."

I'd started my final summer in Wildcat Springs, Indiana, working in his mother Amanda's bookstore. But my life had become complicated, and Amanda had fired me, mostly because she'd sensed—correctly—that her son was getting too interested in me. Even though we'd worked together for a month, Hemi hadn't bothered to tell me he was engaged, though no one else in town had seemed to know either.

However, these events didn't matter. When summer was over, I had one more year at the University of Northern Indiana, and then I was planning to be a newspaper reporter in a city far, far away.

Although Wildcat Springs wasn't nearly as boring as I'd once believed, I didn't have the time or inclination for romantic entanglements when I needed to finish college and begin my career.

Kurt slid my glass across the bar. "What about Duke Talbert?"

"What about him?" Edsel "Duke" Talbert was a handsome investigative journalist and ufologist I'd met recently.

Kurt's icy blue eyes twinkled as he looked at Misty. "Did she tell you about the passionate kiss he laid on her when they were in here together?"

"No!" She gave my arm a playful slap. "How could you keep that from me?"

I felt my face grow warm. "I told you Duke was a player."

"For a writer, you aren't very descriptive." Misty huffed. "How was I supposed to know 'player' is code for passionate kisser?"

Kurt laughed as he walked away to help another customer.

"So how was it?" she asked.

"How was what?"

"The kiss!" Misty shrieked at the exact moment "Pour Some Sugar on Me" ended.

Everyone, including Hemi, looked at us.

Shrugging away my embarrassment, I waved. "Good evening, Wildcat Springs. If you're wondering, the kiss . . . was fantastic," I shouted. "Now, the show's over, so as you were."

A few people chuckled as they resumed their conversations. However, Hemi stood and headed straight for us. Leslie must've been in the restroom because she was nowhere in sight.

"Hemi's coming," Misty whispered.

"I'm not blind."

"Play it cool."

"I don't need to play anything," I hissed. "He's my friend. At least . . . that's how we left it."

Hemi, who was built like a string bean, often wore heinous

bow ties when he worked in his mom's bookstore, but tonight he looked like a normal twenty-something in a navy polo, khaki shorts, and boat shoes. Several people had told me they thought he resembled Matt Dillon, and even I, a longtime fan, had to agree.

"Sounds like you girls are having a good time." Hemi smiled and leaned against the bar.

"Another wild Friday night in Wildcat Springs," I said.

"Who's the lucky guy?"

"Subtle, Hemingway. Very subtle."

"I wasn't trying to be."

"Why do you care?"

Misty elbowed me. "It was Duke." She waggled her eyebrows at Hemi.

"Really," he said. "Are you dating him?"

"We haven't defined anything." The truth was, I hadn't heard from Duke in several days, which was fine, but Hemi didn't need to know that.

"He seems like a ladies' man, so don't let him break your heart."

"Thanks for the advice."

Misty hopped off her stool and stuck out her hand as Leslie approached. "I'm Misty Ambrose."

"Leslie Enright." She looked back and forth between Misty and me.

Leslie was wearing a fitted black T-shirt BeDazzled with teal and pink rhinestones, and she gave me a sideways glance before grasping Hemi's arm.

"Leslie just moved to Wildcat Springs," Hemi said. "She's living with my mother until we get married next year."

Last I knew she'd been working at a summer camp. Had she moved to keep a closer eye on her man? Whatever the reason, living with Amanda Miller would be a nightmare. "I'll pray for you, Leslie."

Leslie squinted at me as if she had no idea what I meant, and Hemi's jaw ticked.

"Are you working at the bookstore?" Misty asked.

"No, I'll be teaching third grade at the elementary school this fall," Leslie said. "This summer, I'm substituting for the aerobics instructor at the community center."

"You and Misty should take a class." Hemi looked at me.

I cringed. "I don't know if—"

"That would be *sooo* much fun, wouldn't it?" Misty clasped her hands. "I have the *cutest* leotard with matching scrunchie socks, because I meant to take a class last year and never got around to it."

"There's a class tomorrow morning at ten," Leslie said.

"Perfect. Bobbi Sue and I will be there."

"Great. See you then." Leslie issued a smile that could only be described as forced, clasped Hemi's hand, and led him back to their booth.

"Wow," Misty said. "That was interesting."

"I can't believe you roped me into aerobics."

"Why? You played softball in high school, so it's not like you don't have athletic ability."

"That's not it," I muttered. "I'd rather not take a class Hemi's fiancée is teaching."

"I thought you don't have feelings for him."

"I don't."

"Then it shouldn't matter."

I stood and threw some money onto the counter. "See you tomorrow."

"Don't be mad," Misty said.

"I'm not. I'm tired." I'd stayed up late the night before writing a freelance article for *Hoosier* magazine, and I'd waited tables at Chuckie's Chicken for most of the day. After losing my bookstore job, it'd been the best replacement I could find.

"I'm sorry for volunteering you." She stuck out her lip. "You could write an article about taking your first aerobics class to encourage more women to try."

"That's not a bad idea."

She beamed. "See? I have—"

"I told you to stay away from us!" A woman's shrill voice reverberated through the bar.

I whipped around and saw Leslie staring down Jennifer Coulter. Since they were both so petite, they looked like two chihuahuas about to nip each other in a fight.

"You're crazy." Jennifer held up both hands. "All I did was say *hello*."

"You did a lot more than that, and we both know it," Leslie spat out.

Misty and I exchanged glances. Jennifer was a pretty brunette, and her miniskirt displayed her toned legs. Had she captivated Hemi's attention?

I could just see the headline now: "Fight Over Bachelor Bookstore Owner Leads to Barroom Brawl."

"Forget it." Jennifer shook her head. "Hemi, I wish you luck. You're gonna need it." She stormed toward the ladies' room.

"What was *that* about?" I muttered.

"I don't know," Misty whispered, "but Hemi dated Jennifer in high school."

"Now that you mention it, I remember, but there must be a lot more going on. It'd be stupid for her to get upset about running into his high school girlfriend." Had Leslie moved to Wildcat Springs because she'd been worried about Jennifer stealing Hemi? "Do you know who broke it off?"

"Hemi. I only remember because I heard Jennifer was suicidal, but that could've been a rumor."

"I hope so," I said. "And to think, Hemi accused Duke of being a player when he's a heartbreaker himself." I rolled my eyes as I left the bar and crossed Pearl Street.

The evening was still warm, and I strolled through the public parking lot toward my parents' tan LeSabre that I'd driven to town. My Escort had four flat tires that I'd yet to replace—due to my lack of funds.

"Bobbi Sue, wait!" Jennifer Coulter waved and jogged over to me with her permed hair bouncing.

Why'd she want to talk to *me*? I didn't know her well, though she'd been on the high school cross-country team with my sister Rochelle.

"Are you okay?" I asked. "I saw what happened in there."

"Yeah." She tugged her T-shirt hem. "I called Hemi earlier this week because I wanted to catch up. I had no idea he was engaged."

"A lot of people are just finding out."

"I made the mistake of leaving a message on his answering machine asking him to dinner. Apparently, his fiancée heard. Talk about insecure." She gazed toward the stream of cars passing through town. "Anyway, how's your sister?"

"Married to Jason McKeever. Pregnant. Happy."

"That's great." Wistfulness flickered in her green eyes. "I wish I could find the right guy, you know?"

I didn't know what to say, since she'd obviously hoped to rekindle a romance with Hemi. "Where are you working?"

"I was a live-in caretaker for Della Jones-Nash, but she died."

"I heard. I'm sorry."

Jennifer pointed at the brick building next to us. "I work at the library now."

"I've always thought being a librarian would be fun."

"It pays the bills." She shoved her hands into her pockets. "Tell Rochelle I said hi."

"Give her a call some time. I bet she'd like to catch up."

"Will do." She fidgeted with her keys.

"You know, if you wanted to get under Leslie's skin, she's teaching an aerobics class tomorrow morning at the community center," I said. "Misty Ambrose and I are going, and you're welcome to join us."

"I might just do that." Jennifer unlocked her blue, rust-spotted Cutlass. "Take care, Bobbi Sue."

———

To get to my parents' house, I had to drive through Wildcat Woods on a winding, pothole dotted road. Even though I'd lived in the sprawling stone house since I was ten, traveling through the woods alone at night always set me on edge, particularly after recent events.

I retrieved a stack of letters from the mailbox and zipped up the tree-lined driveway. Keeping an awareness of my surroundings, I parked the car in the garage and hurried into the house, where I flicked on as many lights as possible.

Nita, my gray tabby, emerged from the hallway and slinked around my legs while I sorted the mail.

No letter or postcard from my parents.

I tossed the bills on the growing stack on the counter and jabbed *Play* on the answering machine.

"Nicki, I haven't heard from any of you since I got back from my cruise, and Judy Beeson told me you went on a vacation." Grandma Spearman's voice reverberated through the kitchen. "I can't *believe* you'd leave town without telling your aging mother. She even told me Bobbi Sue was caught up in a murder investigation." She heaved a sigh. "Give me a call when you're not too busy with more important things than me. You don't understand how embarrassing it is for an old woman not to know what's happening with her own family."

Isadora Spearman had a master's degree in guilt studies.

I collapsed onto the couch.

Recently, my dad's friend Ross had been shot dead at an inn

my dad's construction company had been renovating. Then, my parents had left behind their IDs and credit cards and vanished.

My sister and I thought they'd fled because Dad feared being falsely accused of killing Ross. Years ago, Dad had spent time in prison after a drug lord set him up for his business partner's murder. Eventually, our family friend and reporter Juanita St. James cleared Dad's name.

After I'd helped identify Ross's killer, Rochelle and I had hoped Mom and Dad would come home. But now, I'd have the awful job of explaining to Grandma that my parents weren't on a romantic getaway—they were on the run.

CHAPTER 2

THE WILDCAT SPRINGS COMMUNITY CENTER was in the old elementary school on the south edge of town. After consolidation, the three-story brick building had been closed until about five years ago when the town council decided it'd make a good gathering place. The budget for reopening the building had been scanty, so the council had focused on cleaning and necessary repairs.

I'd always been grateful I hadn't attended school there. After we'd moved to Wildcat Springs, I'd told my parents I thought the building looked haunted. Instead of disagreeing, my normally sensible mom regaled me with the story of how years earlier, a fifth-grade teacher had jilted the custodian and found him dead, hanging from her classroom ceiling. Since then, many people were convinced the custodian's ghost haunted the building.

I found a parking space near the entrance in the back of the building and searched for Misty's Firebird. She wasn't there, so I shut off the car, rolled down the windows, and waited for backup. I wasn't afraid to enter, but I wasn't ready to be responsible for what might come flying out of my mouth if Leslie confronted me about *my* friendship with Hemi.

Jennifer Coulter's rusty Cutlass was parked across the lot in the shade. Women wearing colorful leotards with coordinating tights arrived and hurried inside. With a shrug, I glanced at my sweatpants and Michael Jackson T-shirt that were the best I could do on short notice.

Oh well. I wasn't trying to impress anyone.

A dog's woof caught my attention. A shaggy brown terrier stood poised at attention behind a chain link fence in the yard next to the community center. What'd the dog see?

Then, the dog yipped again as a slim, ski-masked figure dressed in black darted into the bushes near the basketball court. The figure sprinted back toward town while the dog yapped and howled.

I jumped out of the car to get a better look, but the figure had vanished. The dog's owner ambled out of the dilapidated house and yelled, "Arrow, shut up!"

The dog yelped before trotting inside.

"Sir?"

The grizzled man surveyed me and hooked his thumbs through the straps on his overalls. "What?"

"Your dog was barking at an intruder. Someone dressed in black and a ski mask was prowling around the bushes."

"I ain't got nothing worth stealin'." He guffawed. "Maybe someone knocked off the bank over yonder." He waved dismissively toward the building across the street as he went back inside.

"It's Saturday," I mumbled. "Who'd break into a closed bank in broad daylight?" Still, I walked down the alley and surveyed the empty bank. Nothing appeared to be amiss, so I returned to my car.

"Are you ready for some exercise?" Misty rushed over to me wearing electric blue tights with a hot pink, blue, and black leotard and matching socks. She could have starred in a workout video.

"Yep." I leaned into my car, retrieved my red thermos, and followed her up the concrete steps into the musty building.

In the lobby, a wide center staircase led to second-and-third-floor classrooms. To my right was the old principal's office, and Misty led us to the left, past empty trophy cases, toward the gym.

Hemi's mother Amanda was collecting money at an old student desk near the gym's entrance. Like nearly everyone else, she'd dressed as if we were filming an episode of *Body Electric* and was showing off her slender figure. As usual, her makeup was flawless.

"Good morning, Misty, Roberta." She placed some bills into the cash box.

"Good morning, Mrs. Miller." Misty handed over some money. "I'm so excited about this class. I'm sure Leslie will be a great teacher."

"Yes, she's a *wonderful* person." Amanda's gaze rested on me as though she wanted to communicate that I didn't meet her exacting standards.

As if I didn't already know.

"It's good you get along since she's your new roomie." I forked over a few bills.

"Have your parents come home from their vacation?" Amanda asked.

I curled my fingers into a fist. "Not yet."

"Tell your mother about the classes when she gets home."

"I will." I tightened my grip on the thermos and followed Misty into the gym.

On the far end was a stage bordered by a dull red curtain. Leslie had set up a boom box, and the rest of the women were finding places on the gym floor in front of the stage. While Misty and I dumped our purses and thermoses next to the wall and staked out spots in the back row, I scanned the room for Jennifer but didn't see her.

"Good morning, ladies!" Leslie, clad in a lavender leotard, white tights, and lavender socks decorated with purple rhinestones, bounced onto the stage, and popped a tape into her boombox. Electronic dance music filled the space. "Let's start with our warmup. Raise those arms, up, up, up, while breathing in, in, in. Put arms, down, down, down while exhaling, out, out, out." She modeled the moves as we mimicked her.

After our warmup, "Girls Just Want to Have Fun" began playing, and the workout intensified. The moves weren't difficult, but watching the other women entertained me. Amanda was a half-step behind. Misty had an intense look of concentration while her ponytail bounced. Flossie Perkins, a seventy-something retired teacher, was doing an impressive job matching Leslie. A woman with close-cropped blond hair and a teal, belted leotard kept stumbling over her own feet and swinging her arms wildly to regain her balance.

When the song ended, I meandered over to my thermos, guzzled my water, and took my pulse as Leslie instructed. I was more winded than I wanted to admit, so when "Another One Bites the Dust" came on, I held up my half-empty thermos, looked at Misty, and mouthed, "I'll be right back."

I darted out of the gym and into the hallway. While I was searching for a water fountain, a framed black and white picture of a handsome, dark-haired young man with wistful eyes caught my attention, and I stopped and read the inscription on the plaque underneath.

In loving memory of Custodian Phineas Jones (1910-1950). Thank you for your service to our school.

Fighting a cold chill, I resumed my search for the restroom and located a worn sign to guide me. Next to the ladies' room, I found a chipped porcelain drinking fountain, but the water only dribbled into my thermos. Was the running water in the restroom causing the fountain's low pressure?

While I tapped my foot and waited, I perused the flyers on the bulletin board above the fountain. Sunday morning and Wednesday night basketball leagues. A craft club on Thursday afternoons. Sweatshirt decorating on Monday nights. An upcoming cheerleading clinic for elementary-aged girls. An advertisement for next Saturday's Independence Day Parade.

When my thermos was finally full, the water in the restroom was still running. Was someone taking that much time to wash her hands?

I stepped into the women's restroom, but it was empty, and the faucets were off. A quick peek into the men's room revealed the same. Where was the sound coming from? I stood in the hall and listened.

The basement locker rooms.

I'd heard they didn't get used because they were dilapidated, but I'd better check because the town couldn't afford a flood in this old firetrap. I hustled down the concrete stairs and pushed on the door to the women's locker room, half expecting it to be locked.

Instead, it swung open. I didn't find a light switch, but sunlight streamed through a dirty egress window. To enter the locker room, I rounded a corner and took a few more steps down as the sound of rushing water grew louder. A purple rhinestone glittered on the concrete where the flood water lapped over the bottom two steps.

And Jennifer Coulter sagged against a wooden bench with water rising around her.

CHAPTER 3

My first instinct was to leap to Jennifer's rescue and drag her out of the water before she drowned, but my dad's warning from long ago came flashing into my mind.

"Never wade into a flooded basement until you cut power to the house because you could electrocute yourself."

"Jennifer?" I yelled. "Wake up! Get out of the water! Come *on!*"

She didn't stir, and I couldn't discern the rise and fall of her chest. Then, I spotted a dehumidifier plugged into a submerged outlet.

My stomach dropped, and I grasped the handrail and slowly backed up the steps.

Since she was wearing denim cutoffs and a tank top, she must've come here to change, and not thinking about the electrocution risk, she'd waded in to stop the flood.

Praying she'd just suffered an electric shock and was alive, I flew upstairs to the office where I burst in, grabbed the phone, and dialed 911.

After hanging up the phone, I sneaked back to the locker room because interrupting the aerobics class would cause chaos. I hovered at the top of the stairs while the water continued to rise around Jennifer.

I clutched the railing and shouted, "Jennifer, please get up!"

Holding my breath, I waited. But she didn't move.

Knowing there was nothing else I could do, I trudged upstairs to wait in the hallway for the sheriff's deputies, volunteer fire-fighters, and the paramedics. My mind raced, and guilt pummeled me.

Would Jennifer have come to the class if I hadn't opened my big mouth last night? But who could've anticipated this scenario? And why had she felt compelled to stop the flooding herself instead of reporting it to the community center director?

Something didn't feel right.

Then, like a gut punch, I remembered a story my sister Rochelle had told my parents and me one year when she came home from high school cross-country camp.

Rochelle and her teammates were running through the campground after a heavy rain and encountered a flooded dip in the road. A few of the boys were so focused on the idea of playing in the muddy water that they hadn't noticed the submerged powerline.

"If Jennifer Coulter and I hadn't screamed for those dorks to stop, they would've run right in and electrocuted themselves," Rochelle had said.

I closed my eyes.

Jennifer *did* know about the electrocution risk from floodwater, so unless she'd forgotten, she'd slipped—or someone had pushed her.

I considered Leslie's socks and the purple rhinestone on the locker room steps. Could she have shed a rhinestone during a physical confrontation that ended with Jennifer in the water? Or what if the masked prowler I'd seen before class had been involved?

The sheriff's deputies would arrive and assume a hapless female had wandered into floodwater and accidentally electrocuted herself.

End of story.

But my gut screamed there was more to this situation, which meant that as much as I didn't want to deal with Misty's stepfather, Detective Tim Melchor, we needed him. Before I could change my mind, I raced back into the gym where the ladies were exercising to "Billie Jean."

Misty lunged to the left. "Where were you?"

"We have to talk." I dodged a pudgy woman with a side ponytail.

"Give me four more, ladies!" Leslie shouted. "You can do it!"

Misty reached to the right. "Why?"

"Reach for the sky," Leslie yelled.

Leaping out of Misty's way, I glanced around. "Trust me. This is big, but we need to keep it quiet."

She dropped her arm. "Fine."

She followed me out of the gym, and we arrived in the hallway just as approaching sirens wailed.

As we stopped next to the trophy case, her eyes widened. "What's going on?"

Whispering, I told her about Jennifer. "I'm nearly certain she's gone, so we shouldn't tell anyone who it is."

"You're right. The sheriff's department will notify her family."

"I don't think it was an accident, so would you call Tim?"

"What?" Misty gaped at me.

I told her the cross-country story, and she grimaced.

"You have a point, but maybe she's still alive and will be able to tell us what happened."

"I don't think so."

Misty chewed her lip. "Have you completely forgotten my stepdad thinks I'm dumb?"

"No, but if Jennifer was murdered, someone in the class might've killed her. Do we want to let the women leave without the police questioning them?" I considered the figure I'd seen running from behind the school. "While I was waiting for you before class, I saw a masked person running away from the building. What if *that* person is the killer?" I pointed toward the old principal's office. "There's a phone in there."

"Fine. I'll call Tim. But he'll just make fun of me." She entered the office as the emergency vehicles arrived.

"I heard you were the one who found the poor woman. Did you recognize her?" Flossie Perkins approached me while surveying the clusters of women chattering in the parking lot.

All the ladies in the class had been sent outside because the firemen had cut power to the entire building. Not long after, the county coroner had arrived and hurried into the community center.

"I did, but I'd rather not reveal her identity until the sheriff's department contacts the family."

I glanced around at the women. I'd begged one of the deputies to guard the lot's entrance until Detective Melchor arrived. That is, if Misty was able to convince him Jennifer may have been murdered. The deputy had grudgingly agreed and had parked his car sideways to block the exit.

Flossie surveyed me. "You're the reporter who saw the alien in Wildcat Woods, aren't you?"

"Well, that's not the full—"

"Oh, I know. I read in the *Richard County Gazette* about how you helped catch Ross Garland's killer." She stuck out her hand. "Flossie Perkins."

"Bobbi Sue Baxter." I shook her hand. "I remember you from my days at Wildcat Springs Elementary School—even though I moved here after second grade."

"I've been retired for seven years, and I'm not sorry to be missing the things teachers have to deal with nowadays." She removed her yellow sweatband, stuffed it into the tote on her shoulder, and looked back toward the building. "Such a tragedy, but I can't help but wonder if the ghost of Phineas Jones gave the poor girl a shove."

I stared at the elderly woman. "The custodian who hanged himself? Mrs. Perkins, I don't think—"

"Were *you* teaching school in this building when he died?" She put her hands on her skinny hips. "Did you work with the teacher who found his body? Did *you* witness the strange occurrences in this building after he killed himself?"

"No, but—"

"Young lady, I suggest you keep an open mind." Flossie may've retired, but her teacher look hadn't.

Feeling like a naughty student, I glanced around at the other women who were standing in clusters and whispering. "Would you please tell me about that day?"

"I'd be happy to. That is, if you're willing to listen." Her beady black eyes bored through me as if she'd be able to discern whether my mind was open.

"I will. After my experience with the Garland case, I'm realizing that there are strange things in life that defy what we think we know about the world."

"Good. I'll trust you with my story." Flossie stared over my shoulder at the building. "Nella Aidan taught fifth grade, and I taught sixth at that time. Our classrooms were next to each other on the third floor. On the morning of October 16, 1950, I'd come in early since it was Monday. Nella popped in to say good morning, and we chatted about our weekends. Then, when she went to her room, I heard the most awful scream I've ever heard come from another human being." Flossie grimaced. "I hope I never hear another wail like that for the rest of my days. When I ran to help . . . oh. The sight of him hanging there. His face purple and bloated." She squeezed her eyes shut.

"I'm sorry you had to see that," I said. "But do you think there's truth to the rumor Phineas chose Nella's classroom because she wouldn't date him?"

Flossie opened her eyes and appeared to shake away the memory. "Phineas was a friend to everyone—people adored him. Nella swore he never asked her on a date, and I believed her. First, because he was carrying a torch for someone else. And second? Nella was a sweet person, but she wore thick glasses and was dumpy. Phineas was a handsome man who could turn the head of any beautiful woman. He and Nella simply weren't a match as far as looks go." Flossie pursed her lips. "But Nella's word didn't matter. She was the outsider cast as a villain. Folks got so angry at her that she didn't even finish out the school year and took a teaching job back home in Kentucky."

"Did Phineas seem suicidal to you?"

"He was energetic and outgoing, which is why everyone loved him. He had a gorgeous voice and sang Frank Sinatra songs while he was cleaning the building in the evenings. But despite his cheerful demeanor, there were times when I looked into his eyes and saw unspeakable sadness. *I* never had trouble believing he killed himself."

As fascinating as this bit of Wildcat Springs history was, I was having difficulty seeing how this could possibly help anyone figure out what'd happened to Jennifer Coulter. Still, I was curious about the haunting rumors. "You mentioned strange things happening in the school after Phineas died. What'd you witness?"

"Doors slamming shut randomly. Cold drafts I'd never experienced before. Every so often, I'd get a whiff of Phineas's cologne. The lights flickered intermittently."

I shivered. "And this happened while students were in the building?"

"Never," she whispered. "It was *always* after school in the evening."

"And you witnessed all of these events yourself."

"Every. Single. One. I even found desks rearranged in my classroom, and when I asked the new custodian not to move them again, he swore he hadn't touched them."

It wouldn't surprise me if students had sneaked into the building and pulled a prank with the desks, but that didn't explain the other phenomena. "Doesn't it bother you to be in the building now?"

"Not in broad daylight with everyone around, but I'd never been so relieved when consolidation happened, and we moved into the new school." She looked around. "Mark my words, if there isn't a human explanation for what happened to that poor woman, I'd stake my retirement pension on it being the ghost of Phineas Jones." With that dramatic proclamation hanging in the air, she walked toward a group of women huddled under a maple tree.

Misty rushed over to me and towed me onto the playground near a swing set and teetertotter. "Tim and his partner are on their way. He thinks we're overreacting, but I got him to listen when I told him the cross-country camp anecdote. What really sold him was Jennifer's public confrontation with Leslie last night."

I cringed, even though I didn't think Leslie could be ruled out as a suspect. "I don't want to think that Hemi's engaged to a killer." I glanced around. "But there *is* a purple rhinestone on the steps—like the ones on her socks." I plopped onto a swing. "I just . . . feel so bad for mentioning the class to Jennifer last night."

Misty sat beside me. "There are posters all around town, including one on the telephone pole next to our apartment building, so maybe she already knew."

"I hope so." I gripped the chains. "I didn't know she was your neighbor."

"She moved into the unit below mine last week." Misty swung back and forth. "I hadn't talked to her much, but she was always friendly and acted like everything was fine."

"Flossie Perkins is convinced Phineas Jones's ghost pushed her into the water."

"You're *kidding*." She groaned. "Please don't say anything to Tim about that."

"Oh, I know," I said. Tim Melchor already thought I was crazy. "Let's split up, stroll around, and see what else we can overhear."

Misty launched herself off the swing. "Good idea."

We moved in opposite directions, and I hoped Misty would head toward Amanda and Leslie, but instead, she joined three thirty-something women. I caught the eye of the clumsy lady in the teal leotard and was walking toward her when Amanda and Leslie intercepted me.

Unfortunately, there were no bushes close enough for me to dive behind.

Amanda held a small notebook, and I figured she was working on her article for the *Wildcat Wellspring,* our town's biweekly newspaper that she ran out of her bookstore office.

"Roberta, a word please?"

I nodded, though I didn't intend to give her any substantial details.

"Would you state for the record what happened?"

"I left the gym to refill my thermos. The sound of running water caught my attention, so I searched for the source. When I arrived in the women's locker room, I found an unconscious female victim and a dehumidifier connected to an electrical outlet submerged in floodwater. I suspected electrocution, so I called for help." I glanced at Leslie, and she looked away.

A sign of guilt? I caught a glimpse of her socks but couldn't tell if they were missing a rhinestone.

"I have no further comment," I added.

"Do you suspect foul play?" Amanda asked.

"No comment."

"But someone convinced the sheriff's deputy to guard the parking lot entrance to keep us from leaving." Amanda pointed toward the deputy's car. "I overheard someone say you spoke to him."

"I'm sure speaking with the person who made the call is protocol." I looked at Leslie. "Did either of you see or hear anything unusual when you arrived this morning?"

"I got here first at around 9:30 but didn't go near the locker rooms," Leslie said. "I went straight into the gym and turned on the lights."

"Everything seemed fine when I arrived to collect money," Amanda said.

"Leslie, do you have a building key?" I asked.

"Scott Blanchard, the community center director, let me borrow his copy." She fiddled with her leotard. "He told me not to lose it because he'd misplaced his spare."

"Why would he loan out his only copy?" I asked.

"He couldn't be here to open the door because of some committee meeting," Leslie said.

"For the Independence Day Parade?" Amanda and I asked in unison.

"That sounds right." Leslie looked back and forth between us. "How'd you know?"

"I wrote an article about the parade before she fired me from the newspaper." I hitched my thumb at Amanda. "Scott's name was on the list of committee members."

Amanda pursed her lips.

"Oh." Leslie studied her feet.

The klutz in the teal leotard caught my eye again, and this time, she frantically motioned for me to come over. "Excuse me," I said. "There's someone I need to talk to."

I approached the woman, who had tears in her eyes that were framed by a liberal application of blue eye shadow.

"It's Jennifer Coulter, isn't it?" she whispered.

"Ma'am?"

"The victim. It's her, isn't it?"

"It's up to the sheriff's department to identify the body and notify the family."

"I understand." She drew a shuddering breath. "But I walked in behind her this morning, and I don't see her anywhere. I realize now that I didn't see her once class started, and if I'd have noticed she wasn't around, I could've . . ." She swallowed hard. "I'm Tina Ferguson."

"Bobbi Sue Baxter."

This was an interesting dilemma. Tina could provide valuable information, but if I asked too many questions, she'd know that Jennifer was indeed the victim. "Jennifer might've left before class."

Tina pointed at the Cutlass. "Her car's over there. I watched her park and get out. If she's not the victim, where is she?"

"She could've walked home because she locked her keys in her car."

"I suppose."

Her expression made it obvious she didn't believe me, so I decided to ask more questions.

"Do you know Jennifer well?" I asked.

"Not really. We just started working together at the library, and she seems nice." She glanced over her shoulder. "Is it true that detectives are coming?"

"Yes. They're being thorough."

"This wasn't an accident, was it?"

"Why would you think that?"

Tina looked away. "Do you think I'll have to talk to the detectives?"

"They'll want to talk to everyone." What did Tina know that she was afraid to say?

She wrapped her arms around her waist. "If it's a murder, I won't have to go into witness protection, will I? I can't leave my husband—not when I finally found a good man. My first husband left me for a tramp he met at a bar. We divorced, and I met my second husband."

"That's good, but what did you wit—"

"After we got married, we tried and tried for years to have a baby, but it was a difficult journey because I don't ovulate regularly, and he has a low sperm count."

I was about two seconds away from covering my ears. "I don't need to know about your—"

"It bothered him for a while, but when he realized the swimmers he does have are a-okay—"

"Is your husband fine with you talking about this?"

Tina waved a hand. "We're open about our lives. Anyway, we finally had a baby, and now he's eight years old and going to church camp next week. I feel so ancient." She took a breath, and I jumped on my chance to steer the conversation away from human reproduction.

"Did you witness something unusual today?"

Tina swallowed and nodded. "No."

Her head was saying *yes*, but her mouth was saying *no*. *Interesting.* "If you didn't see anything, why worry about witness protection?"

"I've always been a worrier—and overreactor."

And an oversharer. "The detectives will most likely want to know what time you arrived this morning—and if you noticed anything unusual."

"Oh, good. That's easy. It was about 9:35. I know that's early, but I like to talk to my friends, which is why I'm here. It isn't because I'm good at aerobics."

At least she was self-aware—about that. "Did Jennifer have anything to say this morning?"

"No, but I didn't think much of it because I know from working with her that she's not a morning person. By lunch she was always more talkative. Today, she said hello and went down the hall toward the locker rooms. I figured she was going to change, because she had a duffel bag and wasn't wearing exercise clothes." She gulped. "That was the last I saw of her."

I could've overlooked the duffel bag in my panic to help Jennifer, but I didn't recall seeing it in the locker room.

Tina bit her lip. "I hope you're right, and she walked home to get her spare keys."

"Did you find anyone else to talk to before class?"

Tina fidgeted with her belt. "Everybody must've been running late today. I went into the gym to introduce myself to Leslie, but she wasn't there. Amanda Miller came in about ten minutes after me but was busy setting up her cash box, so we didn't talk."

Inwardly, I cringed. Where had Leslie been? A few minutes ago, she'd made it sound like she'd been in the gym from the time she arrived until class started. I'd need to follow up on that. "By the way, do you know what happened to the former aerobics instructor?"

"Oh, I sure do. Shira Elliot's one of my *dearest* friends, and she was getting jowls, so she had a facelift. I told her she looked fine and didn't need plastic surgery, but she wouldn't listen." Tina waved a hand. "At first, she cancelled the classes and felt horribly guilty for disappointing us, but then Amanda announced her future daughter-in-law Leslie was moving here and could substitute. Shira was so relieved."

"I'm glad it worked out." I looked at Misty, who was signaling me because her stepdad had arrived. "Excuse me, Tina."

I joined Misty and Detective Tim Melchor near the swing set. He was middle-aged, bald, and recently, when he'd been interrogating me, I'd noticed his hands were very . . . dainty. After he'd treated me badly, I'd dubbed him Detective Girly Hands.

"What's this about a murder?" Detective Melchor asked.

I relayed my conversation with Jennifer the night before and about the figure disappearing into the shrubs behind the school's basketball court. I even told him about everything I'd noticed in the locker room—including the purple rhinestone.

"I see. And you believe Leslie Enright is guilty because of rhinestones. On her socks." Amusement glittered in his eyes.

I chose my words carefully. "I'm not saying anyone's guilty, but it's strange that Jennifer waded into floodwater instead of reporting the problem when she knew about the electrocution risk."

"Unless she forgot. Or fell." He folded his arms. "We'll question everyone. See if they noticed anything. In the meantime, we'll wait and see what her autopsy shows. I'm only doing this because you were right before." He pointed at me. "But you'd better not be wasting my time."

CHAPTER 4

AFTER DETECTIVE MELCHOR allowed everyone at the aerobics class to leave, I hurried home to change for my shift at Chuckie's Chicken. Even though I'd called and told my boss why I'd be late, Chuckie wasn't thrilled to be short-handed in the middle of the lunch rush. Still, he was fair enough to realize the morning's events weren't my fault.

When I pulled into the driveway, I groaned. Grandma Spearman's yellow Eldorado was parked next to the garage, and I didn't have time to deal with her. Since the car was empty, I assumed she'd let herself in and was probably busy cleaning.

Wondering how she'd take the news about Mom and Dad's disappearance, I entered through the kitchen. Sure enough, Grandma was dusting the living room.

Unless she was gardening, she nearly always wore a dress or a skirt because they made her feel pretty. Today, she was wearing a pink blouse with a denim skirt—and her signature red lipstick. Grandma made it her mission to seek and destroy gray hairs, and the result was that her permed hair was unnaturally dark for her seventy years. Mom had tried to no avail to convince Grandma that a little gray was becoming—and age appropriate.

Before I could greet her, she set the furniture polish and rag on the coffee table and crossed her arms over her ample chest. "What in heaven's name does an old woman have to do to get her family to pay attention to her? I could be lying dead in my house with my cat eating my face, and none of you would care."

"Grandma, you don't have a cat—"

"How would *you* know? You haven't been to visit for more than a month."

"Did you adopt a cat?"

"No, but I should. A cat would love me."

I considered my fickle feline, Nita, who always hid under my bed when Grandma was visiting. "I'd go with a dog if you're looking for love."

"I reckon you're right." She narrowed her eyes. "But if I had a cat, it would chow down on my lifeless face until I was unrecognizable."

We'd be able to identify you by your hair. "But you're not dead, so you could fight off an anthropophagus feline."

"*Anthro-what-a-gus?* Speak English. No one likes a show-off." She snatched the rag and swiped the end table.

"Any cat that lived with you for more than a day would know better than to eat you."

The edge of her mouth twitched. "I'll never understand how your mother raised such an insensitive daughter."

"It's a shame about Rochelle, isn't it?"

"I meant *you.*" She pointed at me. "Your sister convinced a man to marry her, so she's all right. You, on the other hand, show no regard for an old woman's feelings." She huffed. "I haven't heard from you, your mother, or your sister since I came home. I know better than to expect to hear from your father, but you girls? I had to hear from Ina Morrow that Rochelle is expecting a baby! Judy Beeson told me your parents took a vacation, and I thought to myself, surely, my only daughter wouldn't take a trip without telling her widowed mother."

"Grandma—"

"Then, I read the paper and learned about your shenanigans with Ross Garland's murder investigation. Are you trying to give me a heart attack? I couldn't sleep last night for worrying about you."

"Because of a case that's done and over with?"

"You're a lost cause. Who doesn't know how to dust." She surveyed me. "And what are you wearing? No wonder you don't have a boyfriend. Going out in public in a ragged T-shirt and grungy sweatpants."

"I was at an aerobics class." I hoped she hadn't heard about Jennifer's death, or I'd be really late for work.

"*That's* how you dress? I've seen the cute little outfits you could be bouncing around in. You ought to wear them while you're skinny." She pointed at her midsection. "After you pop out a few kids, you'll get a midriff bulge like your mother and me, but if you don't at least try to look attractive, you won't find a man to get you pregnant in the first place."

"Grandma!" I squeezed the bridge of my nose. "Could we please discuss this later? I—"

"Fine. I have other items on my agenda."

"But I'm late for wor—"

"At Chuckie's. I can't believe you went back to working for that man. He's shaped like an avocado."

"*That's* your problem with Chuckie?" I groaned. "I needed a job, and—"

"I heard about you getting fired from the bookstore. How'd you manage that? Spearmans don't get fired. Your grandpa would spin in his grave."

"Then it's a good thing I'm a Baxter."

"Young lady, *everyone* in Wildcat Springs knows you're half Spearman."

"Could we *please* focus on one issue at a time?" I asked. "I'm sorry I haven't called. I want to hear about your cruise—and see your pictures. Do you have them?"

"I'm picking up the slides this afternoon, so you can expect a show tomorrow after you, your sister, and Jason eat Sunday dinner at my house. And I forgive you, dear. After all, I'm a God-fearing woman, and we must forgive those who trespass against us." She sank onto the couch and pointed at Dad's recliner. "Sit. You're making me nervous standing there like you'd rather be anywhere else. How's that supposed to make a grandma feel?"

I obeyed but decided to remain silent since my sparring was making me even later for work.

"Now, did your father drag your mother to a deserted island without telephone service?"

I twisted my hands. "It's possible."

"What's that supposed to mean? Is college making you stupid? Guinevere Brown's granddaughter went to college and lost every bit of common sense she ever had, which wasn't much to begin with."

"I came home one Sunday evening, and they were gone. They left behind their IDs, credit cards, and Dad's license plate."

"Finally, you're making sense." She surveyed me. "Now why were you keeping this from me?"

"I was hoping they'd come back."

"Hope isn't a strategy," she said. "What have you done to solve the problem?"

"Hold on," I said. "You don't seem at all surprised that Mom and Dad fled and went off the grid."

"Of course not. Who do you think provided their fake IDs?"

I gaped at her, not caring if I looked as stupid as Guinevere Brown's granddaughter. "*You?*"

"I have a guy."

"H-How?" This was a little too much to process.

"All those years working as the sheriff's department reception-ist, you get to know people. People get to know you. My guy owed me a favor."

I stared at her.

"Relax. I never did anything illegal. Well, except get fake IDs, but that was something that had to be done. I told God he'd have to understand."

"Why'd you do it?"

"After your dad was exonerated and released from jail, that drug lord who set him up threatened revenge. It's the main reason your parents moved. They figured if they came to Wildcat Springs and lived quietly, they'd be safe." She brushed the dust rag over a lamp. "Is it true your dad found Ross Garland's body?"

"Yes. I think he was afraid he'd become a suspect since he was Ross's friend, which happened. After he and Mom left, Detective Melchor got a search warrant for our guns."

"Your dad wasn't afraid of Melchor. He's a doofus who gets in his own way. I have no idea how he made detective or manages to solve any crimes."

"Doofus? Try chauvinist pig."

"Atta girl," she said. "That's a perfect description."

"Melchor made me so mad, I nicknamed him Detective Girly Hands."

"Even better." She clapped. "His paws *are* delicate, aren't they? Maybe you're not a lost cause after all."

"Don't get too excited. I still have plenty of opportunities to disappoint you."

"True," she said. "Anyhow, it's a good thing Melchor's got Jean Harrell working with him. Now, *she* was a good cop. No surprise she made detective." She stood and resumed dusting. "I'd say your dad split because he was afraid the publicity around the Garland murder might tip off the drug lord."

I hadn't considered the publicity angle, but it made sense. "When they didn't come home after the murder was solved, Rochelle and I suspected that they fled because of the drug lord. But if Mom and Dad aren't safe, what about Rochelle and me? How could they not tell us?"

"They didn't want you girls worrying," she said. "Wildcat Springs was supposed to be your fresh start."

"But it's bad enough that they left us *now*. What if something had happened when we were younger? Were they going to abandon us?"

"Your grandpa and I were going to raise you with your uncle and aunt's help. Your parents never wanted you to live a life on the run. Not when you were kids—and certainly not now that you're grown. My guess is that after your mom and dad learned they're going to be grandparents, they left to put all this to rest for good."

"How are they gonna do that?"

"I don't know. Probably better that way."

"And you really haven't heard from them?"

"No." She held up her right hand. "I wouldn't lie to you."

"You certainly don't have trouble being truthful, so despite the fake IDs, I believe you."

She laughed.

"And to answer your earlier question about what I've done to solve the problem, I called Juanita St. James in case Mom and Dad had contacted her, but she didn't know anything. Or at least she pretended not to."

"That's good. I was beginning to think you didn't care."

I gritted my teeth. "I didn't know where to look, and it's not like I could ask Detective Melchor for help."

"I suppose not, and I'd say the last thing your parents want is you and your sister getting involved, so maybe you're not as insensitive as I thought."

"We've made progress today." I started to stand, but when she made a motion for me to sit, I obeyed.

"Your car has slashed tires," she said. "Did this come from your involvement in the Garland murder investigation?"

"Yes."

"I called a tow truck, and I'm paying to have your tires replaced."

"Thank you, but you don't—"

"You don't have the money, or they'd be fixed, right?"

"Right."

"Then let me do this," she said. "I can't take my money with me, and I don't have a flesh-eating feline to inherit it when I'm dead and gone."

"Thank you." I debated if I should keep my butt glued to the recliner—and opted not to move.

"You're welcome. Now, I saw that pile of mail sitting on the kitchen table, so I'll bet you're worried about the bills."

"Yes."

"Don't be. I have access to an account your parents created for such a time as this. I'll use that money to pay their mortgage and other bills. I'll even stop by your dad's office and talk to his business manager to make sure their construction projects are running smoothly."

"That's a relief."

Grandma guilt was a small price to pay for her willingness to help.

"Go on." She flipped the dust rag at me. "Get ready for work. I don't want my granddaughter getting fired from another job."

I moved toward my room but stopped. "One more thing."

"What?"

"If you knew about the fake IDs and the plan to leave Rochelle and me behind, and you had a theory about what caused Mom and Dad to go on the run, why'd you put me through the world's worst guilt trip?"

She smirked. "Because no matter what, you should always call your grandma."

CHAPTER 5

CHUCKIE'S CHICKEN was hopping since Wildcat Springs didn't have many restaurants, and I made a nice amount in tips that afternoon. By evening, word had spread that Jennifer Coulter died in the community center's basement, and from what I was overhearing, Flossie Perkins wasn't the only one who believed Phineas Jones's ghost was responsible. A few people claimed Jennifer was suicidal, but those who'd speculated about foul play landed on one suspect—Leslie Enright.

Part of me wondered if Leslie was an easy target because she was new in town, and nobody wanted to believe Wildcat Springs was home to another murderer.

That evening, I packed a takeout order for a thin, middle-aged woman waiting near the door. She was reading the *Richard County Gazette,* and when she saw me approaching with her food, she folded the paper and tossed it onto the seat next to her. Her face displayed traces of fading bruises, and her nose and shoulders were sunburned.

"I'm sorry about the wait, ma'am," I said.

"I waited less than ten minutes, so there's no need to apologize. But for heaven's sake, don't call me *ma'am.*" She stood. "It makes me feel old. Call me Shira."

Shira. "Are you by chance the regular aerobics instructor at the community center?" I handed her the sack and walked around to the cash register.

"How'd you guess?" She squinted. "I don't recall seeing you at any of my classes."

"I went to class this morning, where I heard the regular instructor's name is *Shira.* I don't hear that name very often." *And the bruising from your facelift is a dead giveaway.*

"My parents wanted something unique." She removed her wallet from her purse. "I take it you were there when Jennifer's accident happened."

"Yes."

"Jennifer was my mother Della's caregiver before she died. My family and I were boating at the reservoir today, but when I got home, I had a message from my friend Tina telling me all about Jennifer's passing." Tears flooded Shira's eyes. "So tragic—and avoidable."

"Yes, it was." I took the ten-dollar bill she was holding out.

Shira set her jaw. "Not to sound petty, but I know the rubes in this hick town are going to blame the ghost of my poor uncle Phineas."

"Based on what I've overheard today, I'm sorry to say you're right." I took out a penny and handed it to her. "Nine ninety." I gave her a dime. "And ten."

She dropped the change in her wallet and snapped it shut. "No one cares how my family feels. It's bad enough my mother lost her only brother, but to have people accuse him of being a vindictive ghost is downright mean."

"I'm sorry. Were you close to your uncle?"

She glared at me. "How old do you think I am?"

Old enough to need a face lift. "Not old enough to remember him well, unless you happen to be older than you look."

She narrowed her eyes. "I was seven when he died, so I barely remember him." She put her wallet into her purse. "My mom always believed Phineas was murdered."

Interesting. "Why?"

"She talked to Phineas the day he died, and he was looking forward to a fishing trip to Minnesota that summer. Plus, he mentioned buying a house that'd just come on the market. But the biggest factor was that he didn't leave a suicide note. Mom was convinced he would've explained himself."

"Has anyone ever investigated?"

"Mom tried until she was too sick to go on, but she was unsuccessful. To be honest, her investigation helped spur the ghost rumors, so I'm hoping that by my accepting that Uncle Phineas killed himself, others will too." She held up the bag. "I need to scoot before my husband and children starve to death."

When it was nearing closing time, and I was resetting tables because the restaurant was empty, Hemi stormed into Chuckie's and scooched into a booth.

I approached him. "Hey. What would you like to drink?"

"Nothing. I came to talk to you."

My stomach tightened at his clipped tone. Had he heard I suspected Leslie? "What's on your mind?"

"Detective Melchor isn't convinced Jennifer's death is an accident, so he questioned Leslie and told her not to leave town. That moron thinks she might've killed Jennifer!" His jaw muscle ticked.

I slid into the orange vinyl seat across from him. "Because of their spat at Tate's Place?"

"And they found a purple rhinestone in the community center basement that matches the ones on Leslie's socks."

I shifted. "Was her sock missing a rhinestone?"

"Yes," he snapped.

"Lots of women wear clothes with rhinestones, and this morning, I saw a sign about a sweatshirt decorating class at the center," I said. "Who knows how long the rhinestone was on the floor? Or what if Leslie shed the rhinestone that morning in the lobby, and it stuck to Jennifer's shoe and fell off in the locker room?"

"Leslie swears she never went into the basement—or saw Jennifer at all, but there's a witness who arrived early and saw Jennifer. The worst part is that the witness is saying she didn't see Leslie until class started, but Leslie swears she was in the gym the whole time before class."

Was Tina Ferguson lying because *she'd* killed Jennifer? Or was Leslie the one hiding the truth?

I took the pen from my apron and doodled flowers on the menu placemat to help me think. "So Detective Girly Hands's theory is that Leslie was in the basement arguing with Jennifer."

"Right."

"I told Detective Melchor that someone dressed in all black and a ski mask was running away from the school before class, so maybe that person was involved." I leaned back and folded my arms. "Have they even finished Jennifer's autopsy yet?"

"I don't know."

I resumed sketching and pushed away the guilt poking me. If I hadn't said anything to Detective Girly Hands, Leslie might not be in trouble. "Jennifer's death could be ruled an accident."

"I know."

"Melchor needed to question Leslie, or he wouldn't be doing his job. It's possible the witness is lying to cover her guilt." If Tina were the witness, that could be true. She'd been nervous for some reason. "Everything will be fine, Hemi."

He fidgeted with the scalloped placemat. "Mother heard from one of the school board members that they may fire Leslie."

"You've got to be kidding." I bristled, clicked my pen, and dropped it back into my apron. "What about innocent until proven guilty?"

"Some people aren't comfortable with that standard and are

convinced if the police suspect you, you've done something wrong."

I'd encountered that attitude many times before. "Are you sure you don't want anything to eat or drink?" I slid out of the booth. "It might make you feel better."

He shook his head. "Will you help Leslie?"

The earnest expression in his eyes caused an annoying flutter in my tummy, and I gripped the seat back. "How?"

"Do what you did for the Ross Garland case."

"Detective Melchor wouldn't like me getting involved."

"Since when do you care what Detective Girly Hands thinks?"

"I don't."

"Is this about my mother?" he asked. "Because she feels guilty for firing you from the newspaper."

"Yet she hasn't asked me to come back." I folded my arms.

"It's hard for her to admit when she's wrong."

"Tell me something I don't know," I said. "I don't suppose she's willing to say she was wrong about firing me from the bookstore."

He looked out the window. "She just wants Leslie and me to make it down the aisle."

"You should want to marry Leslie without Mommy Dearest's interference."

"Mother just wants what's best for me." He still wouldn't meet my gaze.

"If Leslie's a killer, then, clearly, that's not what's best."

His eyes flashed, and he shot up. "Forget it. If you knew Leslie like I did, you'd realize there's no way she could hurt anyone. I thought you, of all people, would understand how it feels when someone you love is falsely accused of murder."

I put my hands on my hips. "It's about time you admitted you love her."

"*That's* your takeaway?" He scowled. "I'm planning to marry her, aren't I?"

"It would seem."

He strode toward the exit, then stopped. "This isn't just about Leslie, you know. Jennifer deserves justice. And doesn't the truth always matter?" He yanked the door open.

He'd saved his most persuasive statement for last because he knew that was the motto driving my desire to be a journalist.

"You're right," I said. "Wait."

He let go of the door and faced me.

"Why was Leslie mad at Jennifer last night?" I asked. "Because I'm not buying it was all about an answering machine message."

"Jennifer also wrote a letter saying she wanted to see me again."

Now Leslie's reaction last night made more sense, but it certainly strengthened her motive. "Would you mind if I read it?"

"You could if Leslie hadn't burned it, but basically Jennifer wrote about her favorite memories with me as if she were trying to persuade me to give her another chance." He shoved his hands in his pockets. "Leslie might've excused it—if Jennifer hadn't already known I was engaged."

I studied his expression and the turmoil in his eyes. "That's not all, is it?"

"In the short period of time Leslie's lived here, we've run into Jennifer at the drive-in, a restaurant in Richardville, our church, and the hardware store in Wildcat Springs. Not to mention Tate's Place."

"Did you think she was stalking you?"

"It felt that way, but we live in a small town, so it's possible the encounters were coincidences."

"I'd give you a couple. But five? I have high school classmates who live in town, and I haven't run into them once since graduation. And you only saw Jennifer when you were with Leslie?"

"She was at the drugstore on Thursday when I came in. We spoke briefly, but that was it." He ran his fingers through his hair. "Jennifer and I dated in high school, and I took her to prom. She was nice but clingy. Since we didn't have much in common, I broke up with her."

"How'd she take it?" I wanted to see if he corroborated what Misty had heard about Jennifer being suicidal.

"She threatened to kill herself." He closed his eyes. "I swear I let her down easy—and in person."

"Did she attempt suicide?"

"No. She was just trying to manipulate me."

Another wave of guilt over inviting Jennifer to the aerobics class washed over me. But, if she were stalking Leslie and Hemi, there was a chance she already knew about the class and had planned to attend before I'd opened my big mouth. "Okay, I'll help."

"Thanks." He grasped my hands, and my heart fluttered. "And could you do me a favor?"

I tugged my hands away. "I'm already doing you a favor."

"Don't tell Leslie."

"Why?"

"She wouldn't understand."

"Why?"

"Because she wouldn't."

"Wh—?"

"What are you, three?"

"Feel free to find someone else to help." I folded my arms across my chest and stared at him—but he didn't look away.

"She's insecure," he said quietly. "And I don't want her getting the wrong idea about our friendship."

"As. If." I lifted my chin.

He gazed at me. "Are you in or out?"

"In. Anything else I should know?"

"Yeah." He stepped back. "When I saw Jennifer at the drugstore, she tried to hide it, but she was buying a pregnancy test."

CHAPTER 6

SATURDAY NIGHT, I'd considered sleeping in and skipping church the next morning, but now that Grandma was home, I couldn't get away with that. Instead, I got up early and, before the service, drove to the community center to snoop. The day before, I'd seen a sign for Sunday morning basketball leagues, so I hoped the building would be open.

When I arrived, a few guys wearing basketball jerseys were exiting. The light was on in the old principal's office, and a man in a red jersey sat with his feet propped on the desk and a phone to his ear. His sandy colored mullet was stringy with sweat. I pushed open the door and stood next to the reception desk, but he didn't notice.

"I'm playing basketball . . . like every Sunday morning." He sounded irritated as he lifted his arm and looked at his watch. "I'll be home for lunch." He listened. "You've got to be kidding. No, no. I know. We just hosted my brother, so now it's my turn to put up with your parents." He recited the words as if he were a hostage appeasing a captor. "See you later." He slammed down the phone with a growl.

"Excuse me, sir."

He whipped around and dropped his feet to the floor. "Oh, hey there. Sorry if you overheard that conversation. I was hoping for a relaxing afternoon, but my out-laws are coming." He stood. "What can I do for you?"

"Are you the director?" I guessed he was in his early thirties, and his cheeks were ruddy.

"Yep. Scott Blanchard."

"I've been looking for a place to have a baby shower for my sister this fall, and I thought one of the rooms in this building might be ideal." That wasn't a total lie. I *had* been thinking about throwing Rochelle a shower in a few months, though I'd probably use my parents' house to save money.

"I'm guessing you're not interested in the gym and want a cozier space—most ladies do."

"Cozy is good."

"Let me show you the options, and if you're interested, we can talk dates. You'll have to excuse my appearance. I helped my team win a basketball game this morning." He motioned for me to follow him, and I trailed behind his sweaty scent. He led me out of the office and into the hall. "Most gals planning an event choose the library. My wife used it for her sister's bridal shower. It's spacious, and the old teacher's lounge is across the hall, so there's a stove, sink, and refrigerator." He approached a wall of windows and opened a door. "Ladies first."

For a second, my overactive imagination took over, and I half expected to see a custodian ghost holding a mop and floating around in the dark room.

There's no such thing as ghosts.

Scott brushed past me and flicked on the lights. The shelves had been removed, and round tables were arranged throughout the space. The book lover in me felt a twinge of sadness, which was ridiculous because the library at the new school was much better than this one.

"This is a nice room," I said. "Plenty big."

"If it's too large, we have a second option."

I scooted into the hallway, and he led me around a corner and stopped in front of a wooden door.

"This used to be two classrooms, but they removed a wall to make a meeting room." He opened the door and switched on the lights, though it wasn't necessary because large windows flooded the space with sunshine.

A conference table surrounded by a dozen chairs stood in the middle.

"This room is perfect for an intimate gathering." The words seemed a little strange coming from a grubby basketball player.

"I see."

"Would you like to check for available dates?" he asked.

I chewed my lip to sell the hesitation act. "Well . . ."

"Do you have more questions?"

"Is this building haunted by the ghost of Phineas Jones?" I blurted and glanced around with feigned nervousness.

"Hard to say. Personally, I don't buy into that garbage." He looked at his jersey. "But I've always hoped that if the rumors *were* true, Phineas might swoop in and give my shots a little extra help." He pretended to shoot a basket.

"Uh-huh. Have you ever experienced any paranormal activity?"

"Such as?"

"Drafts of cold air? Doors slamming? Phantom smells? Strange noises?"

"I heard strange noises once, but it was bats in the classrooms upstairs, and the only draft I've felt is the one that comes through my old office windows on a cold day." He chuckled. "I don't think you have anything to worry about."

I walked into the hall. "Have the rumors about Phineas been bad for business?"

"Nope." He smoothed his mullet. "Some folks are fascinated by the legend, and others don't want to talk about it at all. But either way, we've had a lot of people use the meeting rooms."

"Good to know." I faked a shiver and rubbed my arms. "Are the rooms upstairs used for anything?"

"Just storage." He pointed toward the stairs. "You're welcome to nose around if you want. The building belongs to the community." He grinned. "You want to see the room where Phineas hanged himself, don't you?"

"Well, I—"

"Come on. I'll show you." He tromped up the center staircase, and we passed the second floor and continued to the third. "Believe it or not, the board considered giving ghost tours at Halloween, but Phineas's niece, Shira Elliot, protested. They backed off after they realized how hurtful it was for his family." He opened the door to room twelve. "This is it."

A green, wood-trimmed chalkboard lined the wall next to the door. Student desks were stacked and shoved into a corner. A teacher's desk was pushed against a wall, and a coatroom was opposite the chalkboard. Three large windows overlooked the basketball court.

I approached the windows and peered out. A narrow path wound between the neighbor's house and the hedge.

Scott tapped my arm and pointed at the ceiling. "This is the rafter Phineas allegedly used to do the deed. Only the third-floor classrooms have exposed beams."

That architectural detail could explain why Phineas had chosen Nella's classroom. But what had driven the poor man to take his life? Flossie didn't believe it had to do with Nella, so if she was correct, what had caused him to take such a drastic action?

"Thanks for showing me the room." I faked a glance at my watch. "But if I don't hurry, I'm going to be late for church."

"No prob." He led the way downstairs.

"It's sad what happened to Jennifer Coulter yesterday," I said as we stopped in the hallway next to his office. "Did you know her?"

"No, but I feel horrible. Normally, I would've been here to

open the building and would've heard the water, but I had a meeting, so I let Leslie borrow my key." He shook his head. "I wish Jennifer had called for help instead of trying to fix the problem herself."

I bit my tongue. "Do you know what caused the flood?"

"A pipe burst. Maintaining this building is part of my job, and I should've thought to check the old metal pipes for corrosion. If I had, Jennifer might still be alive."

The phone jangled in Scott's office.

"Excuse me." He hurried to answer it.

Ensuring Scott's back was turned, I hurried toward the basement to see the leaky pipe for myself. There was a paper on the locker room door that read *Closed for repairs*, but since there was no yellow crime scene tape, I ignored the sign.

The water had been drained from the basement, so I stepped into the lower level. A few puddles remained, and two box fans whirred.

"What happened, Jennifer? You didn't deserve to die that way." I tiptoed past the area where her body had sprawled against the bench.

I surveyed rust-streaked sinks, but the pipes underneath were intact. I poked open three beat-up stall doors and examined the toilets, but they were firmly attached to the wall. Near the window, a corroded pipe with a jagged slit trailed from the ceiling —the leak culprit. I had to admit that nothing about the damage appeared intentional.

Nothing else seemed amiss.

Glancing at my watch again, I hurried upstairs and slipped out while Scott was still on the phone. Church had already started, but if I was there in time for Pastor Bernard's sermon, I'd hear the important part. No one wanted to hear me singing hymns, so I'd be doing fellow church members a favor.

As I walked to the car, Arrow the dog yipped at me from his yard next door.

"Arrow, shut up." The dog's creepy owner was rocking in a wooden chair on his back porch. "You find that intruder you thought you saw yesterday?" Creepy Man shouted and withdrew a pack of cigarettes from his overalls pocket.

I bristled. "No, but I didn't imagine it."

"Sure, hon." He lit his cigarette.

Clenching my teeth, I walked over to the chain link fence, and Arrow greeted me. "Considering someone died in the building yesterday, I wouldn't be so cavalier. What if that person was Jennifer Coulter's killer?"

"Pet the dog. He don't bite pretty girls." He took a drag on his cigarette.

Since Arrow was wagging his tail, I reached over the fence and tapped his head. "Good boy. I'm sorry for your life circumstances," I murmured.

"There ain't no killer," Creepy Man said. "That dingbat female walked right into the water and fried herself." He chortled himself into a coughing fit.

I shuddered at his word choice. "We don't know that."

"Well, one thing's certain." He hacked again. "They shoulda razed the building years ago. Then that old pipe wouldn'ta burst and caused a flood in the first place."

Creepy Man had a valid point, but I wasn't about to let him know I agreed.

"After the cops talked to me, I realized I seen her park her car right under that tree over yonder yesterday morning." He pointed his cigarette at the maple tree. "She got out and trotted into the building like she had no idea her clock was about to run out."

"What time was that?"

"Prolly 'round nine-thirty. Arrow started barking smack dab in the middle of *Muppet Babies*, so I let him out. That's when I seen her."

Muppet Babies? That was a new level of creepy. "Was anyone else with her?"

"Dunno. Went back in to watch TV. Arrow likes to take his sweet time." He hacked some more and spat into the grass. "Why're you nosin' around anyhow?"

The Fruity Marshmallow Krispies I'd eaten for breakfast threatened to reappear. "Helping a friend."

"Huh. Might wanna watch your back." He grinned, revealing crooked yellow teeth. "You have a nice day now, Bobbi Sue." He hocked another loogie and went inside.

Gagging, I got in my car and remembered—I hadn't introduced myself.

CHAPTER 7

"ROBERTA SUE BAXTER, why were you late for church?" Grandma asked when the service was over, and we were stepping into the stifling July heat. "I thought I'd drop dead from shame when you tromped in ten minutes after the service started. Do you want to be responsible for your grandma's untimely demise?"

I stopped on the sidewalk in front of the church. "I ran an errand."

"On the Lord's Day? Shame on you. Errands should wait until Monday."

"I'm sorry."

She put her hands on her hips. "Why on Earth didn't you tell me that you found the poor Coulter girl in the community center basement yesterday?"

"We had plenty of other topics to cover, and your critique of my aerobics attire sidetracked me."

"Hmph. That's a poor excuse for keeping critical information from your grandma. We'll discuss this later. Go on to my house, and set the table for dinner. I need to talk to Judy Beeson." She waved at her friend, who was exiting the church followed by my sister Rochelle and her husband Jason.

After Grandma ordered my sister to check on the roast in the oven, Rochelle, Jason, and I took off on foot past Sycamore Park toward Grandma's house. She lived on Walnut Street, which was narrow and often congested. Leaving our cars at church was easier than finding a parking space near her house.

Rochelle was the pretty Baxter sister because she'd inherited our mom's blond hair and bright blue eyes. Jason adored my sister but was average in looks, height, and personality.

"I haven't heard from Mom or Dad. Have you?" Rochelle grasped Jason's hand.

"No, and if I do, you'll be the first person I'll call."

She glanced over her shoulder, even though we were well past the church. "Does Grandma know?"

"Yep." I told her what Grandma had shared about the fake IDs and secret bank account. "If this had happened years ago, we would've lived with Grandma and Grandpa."

Jason chuckled, but when Rochelle glared at him, I decided to change the subject.

"You heard about Jennifer Coulter, right?" I asked.

"It was all anyone could talk about in Sunday school," she said. "How could you not tell me you found her?"

"Stress isn't good for you or the baby."

She scowled. "Everyone was looking at me like *I'd* have answers, but I was sitting there processing the fact that poor Jennifer's dead. A heads-up would've been nice."

"I'm sorry, but you sound like Grandma."

"Keep it up, and I'll find more ways to sound like her."

I looked at my brother-in-law. "How do you stand her?"

Instead of responding, he chuckled again, and we stepped off the sidewalk for three boys who zoomed past on bicycles.

"But I'll tell you what's bothering me," Rochelle said. "Remember when I went to cross-country camp, and Jennifer and I stopped those boys from playing in the floodwater with the submerged powerline?"

"I do, which is why I thought it was unlikely that Jennifer's death was an accident. She knew better, so unless she forgot or slipped . . ."

"Or someone pushed her," Rochelle said. "I do have to say it's a little disturbing how many people think Phineas Jones's ghost is guilty."

"I overheard at least five people say that while I was working last night." We walked in silence before turning onto Walnut Street. "What do you remember about Jennifer?"

"She was boy crazy," Rochelle said.

"Do you remember anything about her relationship with Hemi Miller?"

"Someone's jealous." Rochelle laughed.

"Not even." I told them about Leslie and Jennifer's showdown at Tate's Place but didn't mention Hemi had asked me to snoop.

"Hemi dumped Jennifer after prom," Rochelle said. "I remember because I overheard Jennifer at track practice telling a friend she'd threatened to kill herself so Hemi'd come back. She was ticked off when it didn't work."

I thought about the pregnancy test Hemi had seen in Jennifer's basket. If she had a history of manipulation, had she been planning to use her pregnancy to entrap a man who'd fought back?

"Something happened on Wednesday when I was playing basketball at the community center," Jason said. "And it might be important."

Rochelle and I exchanged glances because Jason rarely jumped into our conversations.

"What's that, honey?" she asked.

"You know how Scott Blanchard, the director, is on my team?"

Rochelle and I nodded.

"During our break between games, he was kissing Jennifer."

CHAPTER 8

"ON THE LIPS?" Rochelle and I asked in unison as we stopped on the sidewalk and stared at Jason.

"Yes. And he's married, you know," Jason added.

"Duh!" Rochelle shrieked. "I work for his wife!"

We resumed walking in silence. When we arrived at Grandma's gray-green cottage and traipsed up her marigold-lined sidewalk, I finally said, "I'm going to need more details about what you saw, Jason, because Scott lied to my face this morning when he said he didn't know Jennifer."

"And she means details, Jas," Rochelle said. "Don't leave anything out."

"Uhhh . . . well . . . right. Where should I start?" He held Grandma's front door open for Rochelle and me.

"How about with the basketball game?" I went straight to the kitchen, and they followed.

"Okay." He wrinkled his brow and sat at the table in the breakfast nook. "My team won the first game fifty-four to forty-seven. I scored six points. Had three rebounds. Petey scored ten points."

Rochelle opened her mouth, and I nudged her before she could tell Jason he was giving us too much detail.

"Dan was our leading scorer with twenty-one points. Don't

remember the other guys' stats. Oh, wait." He snapped his fingers. "Scott scored four."

"It's fine if you don't remember that part, babe." Gritting her teeth, Rochelle peeked into the oven and decreased the temperature.

"When I went to the hallway to get a drink, Scott was talking to Jennifer."

"How'd the conversation seem?" I opened the cabinet and took out four plates.

"Friendly. A little flirty. She asked him if there were any job openings at the center, and he told her no. I didn't think anything of it and got some water, but when I was going back to the gym, I saw them." He wrinkled his nose.

"Was the kiss passionate?" I asked.

"Actually—no. It was awkward—like he was trying to get away. *I* was embarrassed and got out of there as fast as I could."

I dealt the plates onto the dining room table. "What if Jennifer initiated, and he *was* trying to escape because he didn't want to be unfaithful?" But why would he deny knowing her instead of telling me he'd met her when she'd asked him about a job?

"Could be. He was extra aggressive during the next game. Like he was mad." Jason looked at Rochelle. "I'd be stinking furious if another woman kissed me against my will."

She rested a hand on his shoulder. "Me too, babe."

"Did Jennifer and Scott see you?" I returned to the kitchen and opened the silverware drawer.

"I don't think so."

It was possible Scott had been trying to end their affair the day Jason saw them. But now that I knew he'd lied, I had to reconsider everything he'd told me. What if Scott *had* been in the building that morning to stop the flood, and when Jennifer came in to change, he saw her. She told him she was pregnant, they fought about the baby, and the fight ended with her elec-trocution.

According to Leslie, Scott had given her his only key because he was going to be at a meeting.

"I see your wheels spinning," Rochelle said. "What're you thinking?"

"I need to confirm Scott Blanchard was at the parade committee meeting on Saturday morning." Last month, I'd interviewed the committee chairman, Ray Winston, about the upcoming event, and since he liked to talk, I figured I could get him to tell me if Scott had been there.

Rochelle groaned. "Let Detective Melchor handle the investigation. We don't even know that her death is a homicide. It could've been an accident."

"You're right." I wasn't about to tell my sister what Hemi had asked me to do.

"What if Scott's wife did it because she found out he was having an affair with Jennifer?" Jason found the Sunday newspaper and flipped through the sections. "Was Margo at work yesterday morning?"

Rochelle bit her lip. "No."

"Maybe she came to aerobics class, followed Jennifer to the basement where she confronted her about the affair, and the argument turned physical." I placed the silverware on the table.

"And poor Jennifer landed in the water and got zapped," Jason added as he opened the sports section.

Rochelle twisted her bangle bracelets. "Margo *has* mentioned taking aerobics classes at the community center, but I don't think she's capable of murdering anyone."

"Anyone's capable," I said. "Especially a woman who's livid about her unfaithful husband."

"Tell you what." Rochelle put her hands on her hips and faced me. "There's an easy way to put this to rest. I'm working at the boutique tomorrow, so why don't you stop by to see if Margo was one of the women at yesterday's class?"

"Good idea," I said. "I'll be there after work."

During our meal of slightly charred pot roast, potatoes, and carrots, Grandma hadn't mentioned Jennifer Coulter. When we'd finished eating, Jason, Rochelle, and I lined up on Grandma's couch encased in a plastic fabric protector. She held us captive for an hour, showing slides from her Alaskan cruise. Rochelle and I knew better than to protest because that would've caused her to talk longer.

The second the show was over, Rochelle and Jason excused themselves, but I was stuck—literally and figuratively. We couldn't all leave at once, or Grandma would remind us the next time we visited.

As soon as she shut the door behind Rochelle and Jason, Grandma faced me. "I heard from Judy Beeson you think the Coulter girl was murdered."

I waited for a guilt trip to follow that statement, but when it didn't come, I said, "I believe it's a possibility." I told her Rochelle's cross-country camp anecdote and how I thought that meant Jennifer wouldn't have entered a flooded basement.

"She could've slipped."

"True," I said. "A lot of people are blaming the ghost of Phineas Jones."

"That's a bunch of hooey." Grandma snorted. "Folks need to let that poor man rest in peace. Although, his sister Della Jones-Nash never did believe he killed himself. For a while, she even offered a reward for information leading to the arrest of his killer, but she never had any luck proving he didn't stick his own neck in that noose." She glanced at the grandfather clock in the corner. "I reckon it's good you convinced the detectives to take a closer look at Jennifer's death. We'll have to hope Detective Harrell finds the truth."

"What about Melchor?" I snickered.

"We'll hope he doesn't get in her way." She opened the door. "You're free to go."

I kept my legs adhered to the couch's plastic cover. "But you hate it when we all leave at once."

She glanced at the clock—again. "I also don't like it when my Sunday afternoon nap is interrupted."

"Since when do you nap?" What was going on?

"Since today." She made a shooing motion. "Now don't sit there and pretend like you don't have better things to do than to entertain your old grandma all afternoon."

I peeled my thighs from the plastic, gave her a hug, and hurried out the door before she changed her mind.

"You'd better not forget to call," she yelled.

CHAPTER 9

WHEN I ARRIVED AT HOME, I found Ray Winston's number in the phonebook and gave him a call to see if Scott Blanchard had been at the parade committee meeting. However, no one answered, and since I didn't want to leave a message, I hung up. Then, I noticed the blinking light on the answering machine.

"Bobbi Sue, this is Duke Talbert. I've been out of town on a research trip and got back this morning. I know it's short notice, but I'd love to take you to dinner tonight if you're free."

I didn't hesitate to call him back.

"Are you staying out of trouble?" he asked as soon as we'd exchanged greetings.

"Define trouble."

He laughed. "I watched a story on the Indianapolis news today about a woman who was electrocuted in your town's community center basement—and her death might not be accidental. You wouldn't happen to be poking around, would you?"

"I would." While I fidgeted with the phone cord, I told him about finding Jennifer.

"I'd like to hear more about it over dinner tonight. Are you free?"

"Yes." I tried to sound cool.

"I'll be at your house to get you at seven."

"See you then." Beaming, I hung up the phone.

———

That afternoon, I lounged on the back porch that overlooked the woods behind the house. I was reading *The Cardinal of the Kremlin* when the doorbell rang.

"Who could that be, Nita?" I asked my cat as I passed through the living room. "It's too early for Duke." I peeked through the window to find Misty bouncing on the porch.

I opened the door. "What's going on?"

"I have a *bombshell* that I didn't want to tell you over the phone because I'm not supposed to know."

"Sounds juicy."

"Oh, it is." She pushed her way inside. "I was having lunch at Mom and Tim's house when he got a call about Jennifer's autopsy, so I pretended to go to the bathroom, slipped into their bedroom, and listened on their other phone."

"Nice work." I led her to the living room.

"Thanks." She plopped onto the couch. "First, they confirmed Jennifer's cause of death *was* electrocution, but it's not going to be ruled accidental."

"Why? What else did they find?"

"Fingernail marks on her arm *and* a shoulder out of socket—but not the shoulder she fell on."

"Someone gripped her arm, she tried to get free, and she dislocated her shoulder before landing in the water."

"Exactly, and you'll *never guess* what else I'm about to tell you."

For a half second, I wanted to try, because I had a hunch she was about to say Jennifer was pregnant. But Misty had always wanted to be a detective, and her jerk of a stepfather had told her she was too dumb.

She needed a win, so I couldn't steal her thunder.

"Don't keep me in suspense." I sat in Dad's recliner and leaned forward.

"Jennifer was *pregnant!*"

I gasped. "No way!"

She narrowed her eyes. "You already knew."

"I didn't know . . . for certain."

"Don't ever become an actress." She huffed and stuck out her lower lip.

"Wasn't planning on it," I said.

"How'd you find out?"

"Jennifer was spotted purchasing a pregnancy test in the drug store a few days ago, but your information is valuable because it's confirmation."

She lost her fake pout. "Who saw her?"

"Hemi." I told Misty about what he'd asked me to do for Leslie.

She rolled her eyes. "Let me get this straight. His mommy fired you from two jobs, he forgot to tell you about his fiancée, led you on—"

"You can't lead someone on if she's not interested."

She folded her arms. "*He led you on,* and now he wants you to rescue his fiancée who might've killed Jennifer Coulter?"

"Jennifer was allegedly stalking them." I recounted what Hemi had told me. "Even though Leslie isn't my favorite person, I don't blame her for getting upset, and I'm not convinced she's guilty."

"I don't know. Leslie was furious on Saturday night. She could've fought with Jennifer in the heat of the moment if she thought Jennifer came to the aerobics class to harass her."

"You're right, but here's something else you should know." I told her about what Jason had witnessed with Scott Blanchard and Jennifer and how Scott had lied about knowing her.

"Do you think Scott's her baby's father?"

"Possibly. I'm working on getting confirmation that he was at the parade committee meeting, because if he was, he didn't have the opportunity to kill her," I said. "It's possible his wife did it. Did you talk to anyone yesterday named Margo?"

"No, but I didn't chat with everybody. I spent too long with one group of three because I kept thinking they were going to get to interesting information, but all they talked about were their kids. I tried to contribute by talking about Tricia and Robin, but they looked at me like they couldn't care less because I'm just a nanny."

"You probably made more progress than I would've," I said. "I'm going to follow up with the Margo Blanchard lead tomorrow."

"Good idea. Any new information about the masked intruder?"

"No. When I was at the community center this morning, I talked to the creepy neighbor again, and he mocked me like I imagined the whole thing."

"What a jerk." Then, Misty appeared thoughtful. "You said the person was running toward Sycamore Park?"

"Yeah."

"What if we go to the public pool and ask if anyone noticed the intruder? I know from taking the girls that a lot of the same people swim at the same time every day, and someone wearing a ski mask in June would be conspicuous."

"But it's the middle of the afternoon," I said. "I saw the intruder in the morning."

"The pool doesn't open until one on Sunday, so they have to adjust their schedules. It's a safe bet some of the same people are there."

I glanced at my watch. I had plenty of time to go to the pool and get ready before Duke arrived. "All right. It can't hurt."

The pool at Sycamore Park was full of splashing and yelling kids and surrounded by gossiping moms working on their tans. I'd put on a blue one-piece with a pair of acid wash cutoffs, and reigning Soybean Queen Misty was sporting a neon pink bikini. As we made our way to a couple of empty chaise lounges, the male lifeguard and a couple of dads gawked, and a teenage boy elbowed his napping buddy.

"Should we split up?" Misty murmured as she arranged her purple beach towel over her chair and sat.

I spread out my towel. "Let me talk to the moms, and you can take the lead with the lifeguard. He's been ogling you ever since we got here."

"Really?" She lowered her sunglasses. "Is he looking right now?"

"No."

She checked out the lifeguard. "Ooola*la*! I haven't seen *him* before. I'll be happy to chat with him." She moved to get up.

"Wait a sec." I held up a hand. "We don't want to seem too eager."

"Right." She sat back in the chair, took out a tube of sunblock, and slathered it over her fair skin. "You know, we're like Cagney and Lacey."

I laughed. "Let's see if we can get any information before we make that comparison." I glanced around. To my right, there were a couple of empty seats, but a woman with a floppy black and white hat was sitting in the third chair over.

I glanced at my watch, then waited a few minutes to approach her. "Excuse me, ma'am?"

She looked up from her copy of *Good Housekeeping*. "Yes?"

"Did you happen to be here at the pool yesterday morning before ten?"

She rested her magazine on her lap. "Yes, and we were the only ones here because Tyler *insisted* on swimming yesterday, so I told him we'd squeeze in an early trip before his little friend's birthday party." She tittered. "Tyler's my six-year-old who runs the house. Why do you ask?"

I faked a smile because I was certain 'runs the house' was a euphemism for *spoiled brat*. "Did you notice a masked person dressed in black come out of the trees over there?" I pointed. "Yesterday, when I was at the community center, a person fitting that description was running toward the park."

"I wasn't facing that direction, but that *devastatingly* handsome lifeguard was on duty. He might've seen something." She picked up the magazine and resumed reading.

"Thanks for your help." I returned to my chair and whispered to Misty what the woman had told me. "You're up."

"The lifeguard probably won't talk while he's on duty, but I'll go see if he's willing to chat during his break." She sauntered toward the stand.

He glanced down at Misty before he looked back at the pool, though he did answer. When she trotted back, I could tell from her triumphant smirk that she'd been successful.

"His name's Jeremy, and his shift ends in a few minutes. We'll chat then."

I looked at my watch and drummed my fingers on the chair's arm.

"Take a chill pill, Bobbi Sue." She reclined in her chair. "That's the billionth time you've looked at your watch. And why aren't you worried about a tan line on your wrist?"

"I always wear my watch, so no one sees a tan line."

"You have plans tonight, don't you?"

"As a matter of fact, Duke is taking me to dinner."

She squealed and sat up. "What're you wearing? What time is he picking you up? Do you have enough time to do something with your hair? Paint your nails?" She had the nerve to look panicky.

"Will you relax? There's plenty of time for me to look presentable." I examined the chipped paint on my fingernails.

"You don't need to look presentable," she screeched. "You need to look hot!"

"I'm insulted you think that'll take so much time."

She waved a hand. "You know what I mean."

"Not really." I closed my eyes and let the sun bake my body.

A few minutes later, there was rustling, and when I opened my eyes, Misty was swiping her towel from her chair.

"It's show time," she whispered.

A female lifeguard had replaced Jeremy, who was strolling toward the locker room. I stood and folded my towel.

"Stay here." Misty stuffed her towel into her bag. "I want him to think he has a shot with me, and if I work alone, there's a better chance."

"Poor guy." I followed her across the pool deck.

As we dodged dripping children, the spray from a pudgy boy's cannonball splashed my face.

I swiped the water away. "Where are you meeting?"

"At the picnic table by the parking lot, and I'm serious." She stopped and put her hand on her hip. "You're not coming."

"You can't stop me from skulking around that corner and eavesdropping." I pointed.

"That's creepy."

"Even if you know I'm lurking?"

"Quit using such sinister words." She entered the locker room. "It's freaking me out."

We passed through the musty, chlorine-scented facility, and when we were back outside in the sunshine, Misty sauntered to the picnic table where Jeremy was waiting while I ducked between a dumpster and a cinderblock wall and peered around the corner.

"Thank you for talking to me," she drawled and rested her hand on his arm. "I *really* appreciate it."

"Happy to help." Jeremy beamed at Misty, and though he was cute, he wasn't very tall.

"Yesterday morning, I had the most *awful* experience," Misty whined. "My car got broken into. The thief was dressed in all black and a ski mask and fled in the direction of the pool."

"I'm sorry."

"Were you working yesterday morning?"

"Yes." He had a pleasant baritone voice.

"Did you see anyone matching that description come out of the trees?"

"Have you notified the police?"

Interesting how he'd dodged her question.

"Oh, my case would distract them when they need to focus on more important investigations," Misty said. "You heard about the woman who was electrocuted? I've heard it wasn't an accident, so I wouldn't want the police wasting time on little old me." She stuck out her lower lip.

I rolled my eyes. *Little old me?* I imagined Misty as a Southern belle in hoop skirts, sitting on her front porch sipping sweet tea, twirling a parasol, and teasing gentlemen callers.

Jeremy appeared undaunted. "You're right."

"So did you see anything?" She batted her eyes.

How much longer would it be before he saw through the act? Or did guys actually fall for this nonsense?

He took her hand. "I wish I could help, but I didn't see anyone dressed in black. I had my eyes on the pool the entire time because I have to protect our precious, *precious* children."

There was no mistaking he was mocking her, and I clenched my fist.

But before I could burst out from behind the dumpster and play bad cop, Misty hopped up and wrenched his arm behind his back. "Listen, you son of a motherless goat."

I clasped my hand to my mouth to stifle a laugh.

Misty's face reddened. "You saw something, and if you don't tell me what it is right now, I'm going to yank your shoulder out of socket and leave you sitting here crying like the little boy you are."

Jeremy's eyes widened.

"Tell me!" she shouted.

"Okay, okay," he squeaked. "A guy dressed in black sweats ran into the men's locker room. At least I think it was a man. The person did have a mask on. Later that day, I found black sweatpants and a sweatshirt in the locker room trash can."

"Did you see who came out of the locker room immediately after that?"

"Not at that time. I had my eyes—"

"On the precious, *precious* children," she snapped.

"More like child. It was just Tyler and his mom at that time. She came over and flirted with me."

His story was consistent with what Tyler's mom had told me.

"No one else was here?"

Jeremy tried to wrench himself away. "Positive. Now let go of my arm, you crazy—"

"What happened to the sweats?" Misty didn't release him.

"I took them home because they looked like they'd fit me."

"They may be evidence in a crime."

"I didn't know," he whined.

"Now that you do, you're going to turn them in to the Richard County Sheriff's Department. Understand?"

"Y-Yes. Are you a cop?"

"A concerned citizen." She let go of his arm. "Have a nice day."

He jumped up, ran to his truck in the parking lot, and peeled out.

I came out of hiding. "Who are you, and what've you done with Misty Ambrose?"

She swiped her hands and lifted her chin. "Nobody—and I mean *nobody*—messes with the Soybean Queen."

CHAPTER 10

"I'll have to try calling Ray Winston again tomorrow." I hung up the phone and faced Misty who was riffling through my bedroom closet. "Or I could drop by his farm. The conversation might go better in person."

"Mmmhhmm." She took out a yellow sundress, held it up, and laid it on my bed. "You should wear that. Duke will love it." She walked toward the bathroom.

I followed her. "You don't have to stay and help me get ready."

"Yes, I do." She flicked on the lights. "I've seen what your hair looks like when you curl it." She pointed at the chair next to the makeup counter. "Sit. We don't have time to argue."

"Not until you promise you won't give me pageant hair." I put my hands on my hips.

She took a bottle of Aqua Net out of my cabinet. "What's wrong with pageant hair?"

"Do I look like pageant material?"

"You could be. Now sit. I know what I'm doing." She wielded the curling iron.

"Fine. But only because I don't want you to wrench my arm behind my back, oh mighty Soybean Queen."

"I wouldn't do that to you."

"Jeremy is going to be warped for life," I said. "I can see the headline: 'Vigilante Soybean Queen Traumatizes Local Lifeguard.'"

She laughed and sprayed a section of hair and wrapped it around the curling iron. "I don't know what came over me. I just got so mad that he was making fun of me."

"Ignore what Tim says about you being a detective. I wouldn't want to be a suspect if you were handling the interrogation."

"I couldn't rough up a suspect like that if I were a cop." She grabbed the hairspray. "You won't tell Tim what I did, will you?"

"As if I'm going to run to my favorite detective and tattle on you." I rolled my eyes. "Gimme a break."

She giggled. "So how *are* things going with Duke?"

"We're still getting to know each other, but he called me as soon as he got back from his research trip."

"That's a good sign."

I twisted my hands. "He's very enigmatic, so there's a lot about him I don't know."

"But that's exciting, isn't it? It's like a relationship mystery for you to solve."

"Unless he's being inscrutable on purpose."

"Like to protect himself from getting hurt?"

"I hadn't thought of that," I said. "Or being secretive is part of the act when you have a side gig as a ufologist."

"That's probably true." Misty sprayed another section of hair. "You already know he's a good kisser, so don't overthink things."

"You're right. I'm going to have a nice dinner with Duke." Why was I overanalyzing my friendship with him? The last thing I needed was a serious relationship, and I had a feeling Duke was in the very same place.

That was perfect, right?

That evening, Duke picked me up and took me to Salvador's Italian Restaurant, a new place in Richardville that I'd been wanting to try. It had an old-world Italian atmosphere with a fountain and several private alcoves. The host led us into a candlelit, arched nook with a single table.

"I hope this restaurant is good." Duke took my hands. "Last time I was in Wildcat Springs, I overheard people in Tate's Place raving about it."

Duke was one of the most gorgeous men I'd ever met, with wavy dark hair, hazel eyes that were nearly yellow, and a muscular build that made me feel as if he could vanquish any threatening force.

"It's perfect," I said. "Now tell me about your research trip."

"I've decided I don't want to write another book about close encounters. The witness I interviewed wasn't credible, and I'd like a new challenge. Something out of the ordinary."

I considered the rumors about the haunted community center. "Have you ever investigated paranormal activity?"

"No." His eyes lit up. "Why do you ask?"

I explained how folks were blaming Phineas Jones for Jennifer's murder, the rumors about paranormal activity in the school, and how Phineas's sister Della Jones-Nash had never believed he'd committed suicide. "What if you wrote a book about small-town buildings that are haunted . . . or allegedly haunted? You could start in Wildcat Springs."

"That's an amazing idea from a brilliant woman." He kissed my hand.

I hadn't expected him to take me so seriously. "Thank you, but I wouldn't—"

"Hey, guys!" Hemi said as he and Leslie invaded the alcove.

Bags circled her red eyes.

I snatched my hand away from Duke and rested it in my lap. "Hey."

Duke stood, and Hemi shook his hand and introduced him to Leslie, who barely glanced at Duke and didn't even look at me.

"I'll go with the host to our table." She pointed toward the man who was holding menus and waiting with a patient smile.

"That's fine, dear," Hemi said. "I'll be over after I talk to Duke."

She hurried away.

Hemi glanced over his shoulder before looking back at me. "We just found out that Jennifer's death has been ruled a homicide, so Leslie's pretty upset. I'm trying to distract her with a nice dinner. Have you made any progress?"

"Not much. Leslie has no alibi, which means I need to find who *did* kill Jennifer, and that takes time. I'm not exactly an expert at this."

"I know, but this situation is stressing Leslie out. She didn't sleep at all last night." He sighed. "Please just make sure you're giving this your best effort."

Duke straightened and crossed his arms.

I threw my napkin on the table and launched out of my chair. "What makes you think I'm not?" I snapped. "I spent most of today investigating, and I have two leads to follow up on tomorrow. What have *you* been doing to help?" I put my hands on my hips and glared at him.

Hemi edged closer to me. "Supporting my fiancée while she's dealing with false accusations."

"Then you won't want to keep her waiting." Duke stood, pressed his hand onto Hemi's shoulder, and wedged himself between us.

"Right." Hemi blushed—ever so slightly. "Thanks again for your help, Bobbi Sue. Please . . . keep me posted, and enjoy your evening." He hurried away.

"I'm sorry, Duke," I muttered as we took our seats.

"Don't be. I gather Hemi has enlisted your help in proving Leslie isn't guilty of killing Jennifer Coulter."

"Yes."

"That was nice of you."

"Jennifer deserves justice."

"Is that your only motivation?" he asked.

I placed my napkin on my lap. "I don't like the idea of someone being falsely accused while a killer runs around free."

"Anything else?"

"Does it matter?" I met his gaze.

His eyes gleamed. "It might."

"Then, yes." I curled my fingers around my napkin. "Those are my only motivations."

"Good." He took my hand and kissed it—again. "I'm glad we cleared that up."

***

The next day, I worked the lunch shift at Chuckie's, and I was busing table twelve when Ray Winston walked in with his daughter Georgia Rae on his hip. *Perfect*. His appearance would save me a phone call or a trip to his farm later that day.

Before the other waitress Katie could seat them, I snagged a highchair and motioned for Ray and his daughter to sit at table ten. Ray was a giant of a man in both stature and personality, and he and his dad farmed many acres of land in Richard County.

"Will your wife be joining you today?" I asked.

"Nope. It's just my baby girl and me." He put Georgia Rae in the highchair and smoothed her wispy blond hair.

She looked at me with huge brown eyes, stirring my motherly instincts.

"She gets cuter all the time," I said. "How old is she?"

"Thank you." He beamed. "Sixteen months."

I took his order for a Coke and a glass of milk and scurried away while trying to figure out how to ask about the parade committee meeting. As I filled the red plastic glass with ice, I concluded that I should shoot straight with Ray. I didn't know him well but had a feeling that he wouldn't respond to subterfuge.

I marched back to his table and set the glasses down. "I'm glad you came in today, because I wanted to ask you something since you're on the parade committee."

He tilted his head. "All right."

Georgia was holding her plush baby doll by the arm and shaking it.

"What time was your meeting on Saturday morning?" I asked.

"Nine." He hitched his thumb over his shoulder. "We met at Della's on Foster Street since everyone loves the donuts and coffee."

"When was the meeting over?"

"Around ten thirty."

"Was Scott Blanchard there?"

"He was, but he might as well have stayed home because he seemed distracted and hardly said two words." Ray regarded me with suspicion. "Why all the questions?"

"I'm helping a friend and needed to know where Scott was Saturday morning."

He nodded slowly as if he were putting the pieces together. "You're investigating what happened to that Coulter girl, aren't you? I read in the paper this morning that her death wasn't an accident."

"I'm trying to find out the truth."

"And you're thinking Scott Blanchard was involved because she died at the community center?"

"It crossed my mind, but from what you're telling me, he couldn't have been." I hoped Hemi wouldn't come around today asking for an update about Leslie.

"Glad to hear that. Scott seems like a nice guy." Ray pushed his straw into his Coke. "I do know one thing. Phineas Jones's ghost isn't guilty."

Before I could agree about the ghost, Georgia Rae hurled her doll across the restaurant, and it landed and skidded across Bill Alspaugh's table, narrowly missing his iced tea.

"Sweet baby Moses in a basket. No, no, Georgia Rae." Ray hopped up and got the toy. "Sorry about that, Bill."

Bill chuckled, and Georgia grinned as if she were pleased with herself.

"You're an ornery one, aren't you?" I made a funny face.

She giggled.

"She sure is." Ray's laughter boomed through the restaurant as he dropped the doll into her diaper bag and replaced it with a toy tractor that she pushed around the table.

"I should've started with that." Ray shrugged. "For some reason, she prefers tractors to baby dolls."

"Nothing wrong with that." I took an order pad from my apron. "What can I get for you and your future farmer?"

My sister had just started working part-time at Margo's Boutique in downtown Richardville, the county seat. When my shift at Chuckie's was over, I drove there to meet Margo—and to splurge on a new outfit. When Duke had dropped me off at home last night, he'd asked me out again for Friday night, and I'd said *yes*.

As soon as I entered the shop, Rochelle rushed up to me, leaned closer, and sniffed. "You stink like cigarettes and chicken grease. Did you not even change after work?"

"Yes. I did." I held out a strand of my hair and sniffed Eau de Chuckie's. "Is Margo here?"

"Yes." She glanced toward the back of the store. "We need a cover story."

I smoothed my hair. "I need a new outfit for a date on Friday— and that's not a lie."

"With who?" Her eyes lit up. "Did Hemi Miller break up with—?"

"Duke Talbert."

Her face fell. "Oh. Well, we have some new things." She led me through the store and motioned toward a pretty woman with eyebrows that reminded me of Brooke Shields.

Margo was standing beside a clothing rack, and steam puffed around her as she ran a nozzle over a blazer.

"Bobbi Sue, I'd like you to meet Margo Blanchard."

"Nice to meet you." I held out my hand.

"My sister needs a date outfit," Rochelle said.

Margo smiled. "We just got some cute dresses you'll love. They're in the back. I'll go grab them while you and Rochelle look around." She sized me up. "Are you a four?"

"Yes."

When Margo pushed aside a floral-print curtain and disappeared into the stockroom, Rochelle led us to a section of dresses. "Well?"

"She wasn't at the class," I whispered.

"Oh, thank goodness." Rochelle perused the clothes and displayed a blue tent-style dress. "What about this one?"

"No." I wrinkled my nose.

"It's adorable."

"It'd look better on you."

She held it up to her body. "Jason and I have baby items to buy."

"You know, just because she wasn't at the class doesn't mean she wasn't at the community center," I said. "It has a lot of hiding places."

She hung the dress on the rack. "You're reaching."

"If she wasn't here on Saturday morning, did she say what she was doing?"

"No. And she's not obligated to tell me—she's the boss."

"I thought she might've mentioned it when you were talking about your weekends."

"She didn't, but we've been busy this morning. I need this job, so don't you dare ask questions that'll upset her." She took a black and white gingham dress off the rack. "You're trying this one on."

"Only because I like it." I grabbed a white blouse from the clearance rack that I could pair with a denim skirt.

The curtain swooshed, and Margo appeared with dresses draped over her arm. "I can't wait for you to try these." She dimpled and led me to the dressing room. "Rochelle found some cute options too."

"She has great taste."

"That's why I hired her." Margo hung the dresses on a hook. "I'm going to have to take her on my next buying trip to Chicago."

"Do you go often?" I asked.

"Pretty regularly. I was there on Saturday and found these great new dresses."

"When you go, is it an all-day trip?" Rochelle glanced at me.

"Yes, I like to leave here around six in the morning, shop, have a late lunch, and come home by evening. Would that be a problem?" Margo arched an eyebrow.

"Not at all. I was just wondering." Rochelle smoothed a white sundress. "It sounds fun."

"Good." Margo looked at me. "I'll let your sister help you. Let me know if you need anything else." She breezed out of the dressing room.

Rochelle drew the curtain and we high-fived.

"Nice work," I whispered but then smothered a sigh.

As much as I wanted everything to work out for Hemi's sake, things were looking worse and worse for Leslie Enright.

CHAPTER 11

On my way home from shopping, I stopped at Misty's apartment to see if she was home. She and her stepsister Stacey lived on the second floor of a Victorian house that'd been divided into three units, and I entered the side door and climbed the stairs. When Misty answered the door, she led me into the living room where the soap opera *The Cute and the Cunning* was paused on the TV. A red-headed actor and a blonde woman stared at each other longingly.

She stopped the VCR and switched off the TV. "I tape my soap every day, and I'm behind this week."

"My grandma never wants to miss *Days of Our Lives*, but no one can figure out how to program her weird VCR."

"What's going on?" She dropped onto her couch and set the remote on her coffee table.

I sat on the opposite end of the sofa and told her what I'd learned about Scott and Margo Blanchard. "Just because Scott didn't kill Jennifer doesn't mean he wasn't having an affair with her."

"True," Misty said. "Now what?"

"We still don't know who fathered Jennifer's child, so we should try to figure that out."

"I agree, but maybe she didn't even know," Misty said. "You haven't told Hemi about the dead ends, have you?"

"No." I gave her the scoop about my date with Duke—and what'd happened when we'd run into Hemi and Leslie.

"Oh, boy. He's got it bad for you."

"He does *not*. He's going to marry Leslie."

Misty's eyes gleamed. "I was talking about Duke, but we can talk more about your repressed feelings for the dashing Mr. Hemingway Miller if you prefer."

My face burned. "Duke's the dashing one."

"If you say so."

"Let's stay focused on helping my *friend's* fiancée," I snapped. "Do you have paper? I want to make a timeline."

"Be right back." Misty hurried out of the room and returned with a spiral notebook and pen. "Here you go."

I clicked the pen. "Leslie got to the community center at 9:30. According to Tina Ferguson, she and Jennifer arrived at 9:35." I jotted the times and events on the paper. "It's possible Tina's lying, because Creepy Overalls Guy only recalled seeing Jennifer enter the building at that time. However, Tina could've parked somewhere else, or he'd already gone back inside to watch *Muppet Babies*."

"Okay, that's weird."

"I know. He's not exactly the pinnacle of credibility." I consulted the timeline. "Tina told me that after she and Jennifer entered the building, Jennifer walked toward the locker rooms, and Tina didn't see her again."

"And Leslie claims she never saw Jennifer and was in the gym the entire time before class."

"Right," I said. "But Tina went into the gym to introduce herself to Leslie and couldn't find her. Tina also acted nervous when I talked to her later that day."

"So, whoever is lying might've killed Jennifer or knows who did."

"Unless one of them has another reason for lying, and the masked figure is the killer." I made a note of my arrival time. "I got there at 9:53, and a minute or two later, the figure ran away from the building."

"What time did you take your water break?"

"It was 10:18 because I looked at my watch and was a little dismayed that only eighteen minutes had passed. It was another couple of minutes before I ventured into the basement, but no one else was in the hallway." I tapped the pen against the pad.

"It's probably safe to say the murder happened between 9:35ish and 10:15ish since you didn't see anyone else." Misty chewed her lip. "This doesn't help us figure out whodunnit, though."

"We need to know more about Jennifer's life," I said. "I wonder if—"

"Oh no." Misty shook her head. "We're not doing that."

"Doing what?"

She pointed at me. "Duke told me you know how to pick locks with paper clips."

"When did I say anything about picking a lock?"

"You didn't have to. I know you're thinking about breaking into Jennifer's apartment." She folded her arms. "Kurt's right to call you Bobbi Snoop."

"Clever Kurt." I grinned. "You should date him."

"We're not talking about that right now." She blushed.

"You have no problem sharing your opinions about *my* love life."

"Let's focus on the case."

I smirked. "I was thinking we could talk to Jennifer's brother Monty. He might share some insight about Jennifer's love life." He'd been in our graduating class.

"We could do that." Misty looked as if she didn't quite believe me.

Was I willing to risk getting caught breaking into a dead woman's apartment to prove Leslie Enright's innocence?

The truth always matters. "But your idea is much better."

She stood. "Tim can never find out."

"Hurry *up*," Misty whispered from her post at the stairwell near Jennifer's unit.

"I'm trying. The lock is old and sticking. It's not like paper clips are the best tools." I glanced over my shoulder, though Misty had assured me that it was a perfect time to break into Jennifer's apartment because the other tenant was on vacation, and her step-sister Stacey was working until eight. But there was always the possibility that someone from Jennifer's family would come to clear out her things, so I didn't want to take any chances.

The lock finally clicked, and after dropping the paper clips into my purse, I stepped inside the sparsely furnished unit. The living room contained a single recliner and a TV console from the 1970s. A dinette set with two chairs was pushed against the wall. A few boxes were stacked near the door, and when I opened the flaps, there were pots, pans, and other kitchen utensils. Either her family had already started packing, or Jennifer hadn't finished unpacking.

"What should we look for?" Misty asked.

"Love letters? Pictures of Jennifer with men? A diary?"

"If Tim and his partner searched, they might've already taken that stuff," she said. "But I don't know if they've been here, so let's hurry." Misty inspected the refrigerator which had papers and pictures hanging on it.

The wooden floor creaked as I edged into the bedroom with a full-size bed, nightstand, desk, and bookshelf. The nightstand drawer contained a tube of lip balm, a flashlight, and a bottle of prescription sleeping pills. A stack of books rested next to a lamp, so I picked them up. *What to Expect When You're Expecting. Life in the Great Depression. Making Wise Investments.*

"A little light reading," I muttered as I put them back.

Then, the bulletin board above her desk caught my attention. Push pins held index cards with handwritten notes.

The first card was labeled *Wheeling Brothers Traveling Circus Timeline—1934.*

"A circus?" I read the cards that followed, each with a date range and town.

Gas City, Indiana, May 3-6

Hidden Shores, Indiana, May 10-13

Wildcat Springs, Indiana, May 17-20

Why had Jennifer thought this information was important? I took a notebook and pen from my purse and jotted down the circus name, cities, and dates. "Misty? Did you find anything?"

"Possibly." She bounded into the room, screeched to a halt, and pointed at the index cards. "What're those?"

"A traveling circus timeline."

"Weird."

"I know," I said. "What'd you get?"

She handed me a picture of Jennifer and an attractive, but older, man with a Magnum P.I. mustache. He had his arm around her, and they appeared happy. "It was on the fridge. Do you recognize him?"

"No. Maybe *he's* her baby's father." I gave Misty the picture and picked up a packet of photos that'd been developed at the local drugstore. They were family Christmas pictures along with two pictures from her family's Easter gathering, but there weren't any with the mustachioed man.

Misty shuffled through a stack of Jennifer's cancelled checks that'd been sitting on top of her desk.

"Uh, Bobbi Sue. Take a look." Misty held out a check for thirty dollars made out to *Isadora Spearman.* "Do you know why Jennifer paid your grandma?"

I took the check and flipped it over. Grandma had definitely endorsed it. "No idea. We'll have to go—"

The apartment door rattled, and we exchanged wild glances before diving into a closet that was barely big enough for both of us. I eased the door shut but didn't have room to latch it.

"Oh my gosh." Misty clutched my arm and whispered, "If that's Tim and his partner, we're in so much trouble."

"Hush."

Her elbow poked my side.

"Ouch."

"Sorry."

I held my breath as footsteps sounded in the living room, followed by opening and closing of cabinets. Then, someone entered the bedroom. Pushing aside a shirt, I pressed my face against the woodwork and peered through the crack at the elderly, dark-haired woman perusing Jennifer's bookshelf.

It was Grandma Spearman.

CHAPTER 12

"Grandma?" I stepped out of the closet with Misty on my heels. "What're you doing?"

She whipped around, clutching her chest. "Roberta Sue Baxter! What in the Sam Hill are you doing? Do you not have a lick of common sense? You could've killed me, scaring me like that, but I suppose you wouldn't even care. You'd have one less person to check on. Although, it'd be better to drop dead of a heart attack in a dead girl's apartment than to keel over at home and have an anthropomorphic cat eat my face."

"Anthropophagus." I choked back a giggle.

"That's what I said." She put her hands on her hips. "You're never going to find a husband if you contradict people all the time."

"That didn't keep Grandpa from marrying you."

"Hmph." She took an old photo album from Jennifer's shelf and tucked it into the tote bag hanging on her shoulder. "What's that paper you've got?"

"A check Jennifer made out—to you."

"I'll explain later." Grandma snatched it from my hand and slipped it underneath the stack of cancelled checks on Jennifer's desk before turning to Misty. "What do you have there?"

Misty held up the photo. "Do you know this guy?"

Grandma squinted at it. "Nope. Now put that back where you got it, and let's get the heck out of Dodge."

"You can't take that album." I pointed at Grandma's tote.

"I can, and I will. Jennifer was borrowing it from me, and I'm not leaving my precious photos here to get donated along with her worldly goods. I tried to come and get it yesterday afternoon, but her folks were here packing."

"You couldn't have just asked them for the album?" I asked.

"I don't want to get mixed up in any of this mess."

So you thought you'd break into her apartment instead? "I knew when you kicked me out you weren't going to take a nap."

"I don't understand what's happening." Misty looked back and forth between us.

"What's happening is that we're getting out of here before someone catches us." Grandma captured Misty and me by the arms and hauled us toward the door.

"I-I need to put the picture back," Misty whimpered.

"Hurry up, then." Grandma let go of Misty but kept her claws on me.

Misty scampered to the fridge, hung the photo, and scrambled back to the door where Grandma snared her arm again and steered her outside. Misty pointed at the ceiling. "I live upstairs."

"I know." She didn't let go of Misty as we traipsed downstairs.

"It'll look suspicious if someone sees you dragging us out of this building," I said.

She stopped next to the staircase and released her grip. "Wait a couple of minutes after I leave. Then come to my house if you want more info. Understand?"

"Yes, ma'am." Misty's voice trembled.

Without waiting for my answer, Grandma hustled out the door to her car.

"I don't know what just happened." Misty leaned against the

banister and rubbed at the red marks Grandma's grip had left on her arm.

"Neither do I."

———

Grandma had a plate of Oreos and two napkins waiting on her coffee table when we arrived. "Do either of you girls want milk?"

"Yes, please," I said.

"I'll just have water," Misty said.

Grandma blinked at Misty. "Water. With Oreos." She clacked her tongue. "Wouldn't be my choice, but one glass of Wildcat Springs's finest tap water coming right up." She hustled to the kitchen.

Misty perched on Grandma's plastic-covered couch. "Is she always like this?"

"Do I frequently catch her entering a murder victim's apartment to steal back a photo album she loaned? No."

"I mean is she normally this aggressively honest?" Misty whispered as she reached for a cookie.

"Every day of her life."

"Huh." Misty twisted an Oreo and popped half into her mouth.

"What?"

She crunched on her cookie. "This helps me understand you even more."

"It explains volumes, doesn't it?"

Grandma emerged from the kitchen and was holding glasses of milk and water, which she set on coasters on the coffee table. Then, she eased into her recliner and extended the footrest. "Why were you two snooping in Jennifer's apartment?"

"Why'd Jennifer have your photo album?" I asked.

Grandma folded her arms across her chest. "We both know you're going to answer your elderly grandmother's question first, so let's skip the sparring." She looked at Misty. "She's a slow learner."

Misty shoved an entire Oreo into her mouth and picked up her water glass.

"Hemi Miller asked me to prove that his fiancée Leslie Enright had nothing to do with Jennifer's death," I said.

"The asparagus-shaped kid?" Grandma sniffed. "Who works in the bookstore with his shrew of a mother?"

Misty sprayed water. "Sorry. Sorry. I'm so sorry." She ran her hands over the plastic cover to rid it of water droplets and Oreo crumbs.

"Relax. You can't hurt that old thing." Grandma waved a hand and stared at me. "Why are you friends with the asparagus spear? His mother fired you."

"*Asparagus spear?* Why are you comparing his body to a vegetable?" I scowled.

"I don't always use veggies. Fruit works too." She pointed to herself. "I'm an unashamed apple. So's your mother. You will be too, someday. Might as well accept it now."

"A pear shape is probably in my future," Misty added.

"There's no 'probably' if you keep eating Oreos like it's your job," Grandma said.

Misty reached for yet another cookie.

I threw my hands in the air. "In spite of his mother, Hemi and I get along, and since I know what it's like to have a loved one be falsely accused, I agreed to help."

"You mean you agreed to put yourself in danger for a man who's marrying someone else but that you must have feelings for, or you wouldn't have gotten hot and bothered over my asparagus comment."

"I don't have feelings for him. I just think it's rude to compare people to vegetables." I vowed never again to think of Hemi as a string bean.

"You didn't mind when I compared Chuckie to an avocado."

"An avocado is a fruit."

"Yes, that makes all the difference," Grandma said.

Misty pressed her hand to her mouth and gulped.

"Are you going to tell me why Jennifer paid you thirty dollars and borrowed your album?" I asked.

"The check was payment for my old camera," she said. "I struck up a conversation with her at the beauty salon when we were getting perms before I went on my cruise." She patted her hair. "I told her about my cruise and how I'd bought a new camera. She asked what I planned to do with the old one, and when I told her I didn't know, she said she needed one and made me an offer I couldn't refuse. I wanted extra souvenir money."

"Did you keep the strap?" I asked. "Rochelle and I picked it out for you when Mom and Dad bought that camera for your birthday." It was woven in a blue and white floral pattern.

"I couldn't sell her a camera without a strap, could I?"

"I suppose not, but did you at least keep the *World's Best Grandma* pin we attached to it?"

"I didn't know you were so sentimental." She brushed some lint from her skirt.

"And you call *me* insensitive," I muttered as I dunked an Oreo into my milk.

"Why'd you loan Jennifer your album?" Misty asked.

"That day at the salon, Jennifer was reading a library book about the Great Depression, so I asked why. Apparently, she was writing a novel set in the 1930s, and I told her I could give her plenty of first-hand information since I lived through it. That's when she asked if I remembered the Wheeling Brothers Circus coming to town in 1934."

"Because her novel was about a traveling circus?" I asked.

"Right. Anyhow, I told her all about it and said I even had pictures. She asked to borrow them, and I didn't see why not."

"Did she say anything else about her novel?" Misty reached for another Oreo, but when she caught Grandma staring at her, she snapped back and sat on her hand.

"It was a mystery," Grandma said. "Something about one of the circus performers robbing the people who attended."

"Did that happen when the circus came to Wildcat Springs?" I asked.

Grandma chuckled. "No. That would've caused a sensation, especially during the depression."

"May I see the album?" I asked.

Grandma retrieved it from her shelf, handed it to me, and motioned for me to make room for her on the couch. As soon as I cracked open the emerald-colored book embossed with gold, Grandma launched into detailed descriptions about each photo while Misty sneaked more Oreos.

Finally, we reached the three pictures Grandma had from the circus. One was with her little sister Adele, and they were standing in front of a striped tent. In another, there was a bearded man on stilts, and in the third photo, a pretty woman in a fancy costume was sitting on a horse.

Grandma pointed at the photo. "Adele wanted to be an equestrian performer like this woman—until she met your great uncle Carl."

"Being a circus performer probably seemed glamorous and exciting," Misty said.

"That's right. This circus was the highlight of our year."

I closed the album. "This has been an interesting peek into Jennifer's life, but it's not getting us any closer to figuring out why she was killed. Do you mind if I hang onto this for now?"

"As long as you don't forget to return it like the hat I let you borrow for your Halloween costume." Grandma pursed her lips.

"I eventually gave it back. It's not like you needed a 1940s hat in 1979."

"I might've. Fashion is cynical."

Misty looked puzzled as she snatched another Oreo.

"You mean *cyclical?*" I asked.

"That too," Grandma said. "Now, what else have you figured out since you've been nosing around in Jennifer's business?"

I told her about Jennifer's alleged affair with Scott Blanchard and how I'd ruled him out—as well as his wife Margo. "However, we don't know who the man from the photo on the refrigerator is, I still need to identify the mysterious masked figure, and unfortunately, I haven't found a single piece of evidence that clears Leslie's name."

"Hmph." Grandma picked up the remote and turned on her TV. "Or you're not going to because Leslie really did see an opportunity to give poor Jennifer a shove."

"I feel like I survived a war," Misty said as we trudged down the sidewalk on our way back to her apartment.

"You get used to it," I said. "Eventually, encounters with Grandma only feel like battles instead of wars."

"I'm not sure I'll live long enough to get to that point." Misty groaned and clutched her stomach. "Never let me eat that many Oreos again. I feel like I'm gonna ralph."

"I was too busy trying to fend off Grandma. Why'd you eat so many?"

"She made me so nervous that I lost my mind." We stopped in front of Misty's apartment building. "I'm going to rest, but if I feel better, I'll give you a call and we can go to Tate's Place tonight." With her hand pressed to her mouth, she hurried inside, and I got into my parents' car and contemplated my next move.

Jennifer had worked at the library, so maybe one of her colleagues could give me more information about her life and her novel research. It was certainly worth a shot.

I drove across town, and when I entered the library, a sour-faced, elderly man was working behind the circulation desk. I had a sudden mental picture of him roaming the stacks, shushing patrons, and taking a ruler to naughty children's knuckles. I probably wouldn't get very far talking to him, but I had to try.

"Excuse me, sir." I approached the circulation desk and kept my knuckles out of reach.

He looked up, and the nametag pinned to his gray cardigan read *Oliver*.

"I'm Bobbi Sue Baxter, and I'm investigating Jennifer Coulter's death. May I ask a few questions?"

"Yes."

"How long had Jennifer worked at this library?"

"A couple of months." He picked up a card pocket and book.

"Were you aware that she was writing a novel?"

"No."

"Do you know who she was dating?" Why was I bothering to ask him that?

He glued the pocket into the book. "No."

"Did she seem troubled about anything prior to her death?"

"No."

I tried not to roll my eyes as I envisioned the headline: "Taciturn Librarian Impedes Murder Investigation."

"Is there anyone else who works here who could give me information about Jennifer?" I asked.

He pointed behind me where Tina Ferguson was shelving books.

"Thanks for your help."

Oliver issued a curt nod.

When I got closer to Tina, she tightened her grip on *Cujo* and issued a smile, though it didn't reach her purple-eyeshadow-caked eyes.

"Is there something I can help you find?" she asked.

"I'm looking for more information about Jennifer Coulter since she worked here."

"I read in the newspaper that her death wasn't an accident." Tina gulped. "What do you want to know?"

For a second, I considered mentioning her claim about not seeing Leslie in the gym, but I wanted to see what else she'd tell me and couldn't afford to spook her. "Did Jennifer ever mention who she was dating?"

Tina ran her finger over the book's binding. "She complained a lot about not being able to find a good man, and believe me, I understand that after what I went through with my first husband. After we split, I dated so many losers—"

"Did you ever see her with anyone?"

"No."

"Did Jennifer talk to you about the novel she was writing?"

"Not much." Tina shelved the Stephen King book. "But we hadn't worked together very long, so I wouldn't expect that she'd tell me her business. One night, she stayed after work and researched in the basement archives, and she mentioned it was for a novel she was brainstorming."

"So she wasn't writing yet."

"I don't know, but she made it sound like she needed to research some possible ideas first. She acted like she didn't want to say much more, so I didn't press her." She took a book from the cart, but it slipped out of her hand and hit the floor.

"Are you okay?" I swiped up the book and handed it to her.

"Yes. I'm just clumsy." She gripped the book cart. "Jennifer had a desk in the back room you could look at."

I glanced over my shoulder. "What would Oliver say?"

"Nothing—as long as you don't talk to him or disturb his work," she whispered. "On my first day, he yelled at me for making small talk, and ever since, I've been terrified of him. It's hard for me to keep quiet, but I need this job because my husband was laid off a few weeks ago, and we don't have any savings because we spent it all on fertility treatments years ago." She motioned for me to follow. "Come on. Oliver's got a line of patrons and will be distracted for a while. Just . . . *don't talk*."

I trailed along, but my thongs' flipping and flopping sounded like gunshots in the tomb-like library, so I slipped them off and followed Tina.

She led me around the room's perimeter to a small office where she pointed to a wooden desk in the corner near a window. "Jennifer's family hasn't come to clean it out. Although, there may not be much in there." She glanced over her shoulder and left me alone.

The desk's surface was empty, and I checked the middle drawer and found the usuals: pens, pencils, notepads, tape, a stapler, and staples. The top side drawer held a half-empty sleeve of crackers and an unopened roll of mints. The bottom drawer was empty except for a green, spiral-bound notebook with Jennifer's name printed on the cover, but when I opened it, the pages were blank.

I held the page toward the light to look for handwriting impressions but couldn't see any. When I replaced the notebook, a yellowed paper slipped out. I unfolded it and read.

July 18, 1934

My dearest Phineas,

I'm sorry I haven't corresponded sooner, but I haven't forgotten my promise to return to Wildcat Springs. William is keeping a close eye on me, and I had to sneak away to write this letter. Please don't write back because he must never know the secret with which I have entrusted you. It is my only hope of having my freedom someday. Please know that I love you and can't wait to see you in the fall.

All my love,
Nadia

Questions darted around my mind. Why did Jennifer have Phineas's letter in her notebook? She'd been a caregiver for Phineas's sister Della before she died. Had Della passed on the letter? Then, I remembered Flossie Perkins had told me she believed Phineas had been carrying a torch for someone. Was Nadia that woman?

Whatever the case, this letter could be too important to leave in the drawer.

I double checked the notebook's pages before putting it back. Tucking the letter into my bag, I decided to give the letter to Detective Harrell—after I copied it.

I slipped on my thongs and exited as quietly as possible, but Oliver didn't look up. Tina was still shelving books. When I was getting into the car, a figure dressed in a black ski mask and black sweats darted out from between the two houses across the street and bolted down the sidewalk.

Before I could change my mind, I adjusted my grip on my purse and sprinted across the street in pursuit.

CHAPTER 13

WHILE I CHASED the chubby figure, I wished I'd run track like Rochelle instead of playing softball. Even though my footwear flipped, flopped, and slipped with each stride, I was closing in on the runner. I hadn't remembered the person's figure being so pudgy.

"Stop! I want to talk to you!"

This seemed to motivate the runner, and he or she accelerated.

"Please, I just want to talk."

But the runner didn't listen.

Digging deep, I pushed forward, reached for the person's sweatshirt collar, and yanked the runner backward.

"Let me go!" a woman shrieked.

I ripped off the mask and chuckled. The high-pitched voice belonged to Dusty Warner—an eleven-year-old boy who attended my church.

"Let . . . me . . . go, or I'll scream." Between huffing and puffing, he squirmed and wielded a paper throwing star as his sweaty hair stood on end.

"Dusty, it's Bobbi Sue . . . from church." I tried to catch my breath. "I need . . . to ask you some questions."

He stopped wriggling and looked at me again. "Oh . . . hi. I thought you were a kidnapper." His freckled cheeks flushed.

With my heart still chugging, I released him, pushed my purse strap back onto my shoulder, and folded my arms across my chest. "What're you doing running around in a ski mask in this heat? You know that makes you look like a thief, right?"

He shifted back and forth. "I'm a ninja, and I'm on my way to my friend Ryan's house. He's a ninja too. Well, he will be if he found a new ninja-yoroi." I must've look puzzled because Dusty added, "His ninja gear."

"Black sweats and a ski mask?"

"Yeah. He lost his on Saturday."

"That's too bad. How'd that happen?"

"We went to his girlfriend Sarah's house to show her our gear. I was hiding out in the bushes because I don't like to watch them kissing." Dusty made a gagging noise. "Sarah's dad caught them, and he was really, really, really mad, so he chased Ryan to find out who he was. I ran the other way and went home. Sarah's dad's fat, so Ryan got away and hid in the pool locker room. He took off his ninja-yoroi and put it in the trash to hide it, but when he went back later, it was gone."

Sweat dribbled down my back. "Does Sarah live near the community center?"

"Across the street. How'd you know?"

"I saw Ryan running away. Is he tall and skinny?"

"Yeah."

"This happened Saturday morning, right?"

"Yep. Can I go now?"

I held out his mask. "Go have fun, and I'm sorry for scaring you."

He yanked the mask from my hand and lifted his chin. "I wasn't scared. I could've fought you off." He donned his mask and darted away, apparently unconcerned about Sarah's dad, who was probably on the lookout for the kiss-stealing ninja.

On my way out of town, I stopped at Miller's Books. Even though Amanda had fired me, I still loved the store because it was full of one of my favorite things—books. When I entered, Hemi was working behind the checkout counter, and several shoppers were browsing the shelves.

He was wearing a bow tie with an electric blue triangle pattern, and his face lit up when I approached. "What brings you by?"

I withdrew Phineas's letter from my purse. "I found this letter in Jennifer's desk at the library, and it could be important to her case. Would you be willing to make a photocopy for me—before I give it to Detective Harrell?"

"If it might help Leslie, then absolutely." He took the letter and stepped out from behind the counter. "George?"

A kid with aviator-framed glasses turned from a magazine rack he was stocking. "Yes, sir?"

"Will you watch the register?"

"Yes, Mr. Miller." George put the magazines aside and trotted over to the cash register.

"Mother's not here," Hemi said to me. "So come on back. I've been meaning to call you."

I followed him to the office where he opened the photocopier and put the letter on the glass. "Have you made any progress?" He punched some buttons and faced me.

I opened my mouth to answer but snapped it shut. How could I tell him that his fiancée was looking more and more guilty? "Slow progress. I'm hoping the letter will help."

"But can you rule out Leslie?"

"Not yet. I'm sorry."

He held out the copy. "I know Leslie isn't your favor—"

"Let me just stop you right there." I snatched the paper. "I've spent all afternoon following leads but none of them prove

Leslie's innocence, so I'm trying to learn as much as I can about Jennifer's life."

He handed me the letter. "Has that helped?"

I bristled and tucked the copy and original into my purse. "No."

"What about the masked figure you saw running from the community center Saturday morning?"

"It was an eleven-year-old ninja." I told Hemi the whole story.

His eyes twinkled. "I'd have paid good money to see you chasing that kid."

"That would've been a complete waste of your resources."

His amused expression grew serious. "But you haven't found anything else that makes her look guiltier, right?"

"Are you starting to doubt her innocence?" I asked.

"You know that's not what I meant," he snapped.

"You don't have to be a jerk about it, and may I remind you that you're the one who came to me. Do you still want my help or not?"

"I do." His tone softened, and he stepped closer. "And I'm sorry. I know I can count on you to find the truth."

My tummy fluttered. "But what if this time I can't? I'm not giving up, but—"

"I trust you." His gaze traveled to my lips.

For a second, I imagined what it would be like to kiss him, but I pushed the thought away and tried to focus on the case. "That's good. After all, I do owe you since you came to my rescue—"

"Hemi?" Leslie hovered in the doorway and looked back and forth between us. "George said you were back here, but he didn't mention Bobbi Sue." She glared at me. "What's going on?"

Hemi blushed and took a step away from me, but I wasn't going to act guilty when all I was doing was trying to help her— even if she didn't know.

"I'll let Hemi explain since I need to go," I blurted. "Thanks for making the copy, Hemi. It's nice to see you again, Leslie."

I bolted out of the office and hustled to the bookstore's exit before Hemi or Leslie could say another word.

CHAPTER 14

When I arrived at home, Eduardo Escort was parked in the driveway and had four new tires. I called Grandma and thanked her for paying for repairs and then scrounged up some scrambled eggs and bacon for dinner. I'd just put my plate in the dishwasher when the doorbell rang, and when I peeked through the window, Leslie was standing on the porch.

This confrontation was bound to happen sooner or later. I might as well face it now.

"Hey," I said as I opened the door.

"I'm not mad," she said. "May I come in and talk? Please?"

"Sure." I stepped aside. "We could sit out on the back deck since it's a nice evening."

"That's fine."

"Would you like anything to drink? We have Cokes. Water."

"No, thank you." She followed me through the house and outside where she dropped into a chaise lounge and stared out into the woods.

I sat beside her. "What's on your mind?"

For a moment, only the sound of bugs sizzling in the zapper broke the silence.

"I don't love him," she said. "I mean, I love him. He's great. I'm just not *in* love with him."

It took me a second to get my bearings, because this wasn't how I'd anticipated Leslie initiating the conversation. "We're talking about Hemi, right?"

Leslie gaped at me as if I were dense. "Who else would I be talking about?"

"Just checking," I said. "I didn't think you'd be *discussing* your relationship with me at all." I'd been expecting a stay-away-from-my-fiancé manifesto.

"You're friends with him, right? He *finally* told me he asked you to help clear my name, which is so sweet of both of you." She squeezed the bridge of her nose.

"He's worried."

"I know, and that's one more thing I feel guilty about."

"Why?"

"I can't exactly tell him that there's no way I killed Jennifer because I don't love him enough to kill for him."

I was having trouble processing this information and was more than a little disturbed at the implication that there was a man out there that this tiny elementary school teacher *would* kill for. "But you yelled at Jennifer at the bar, and everyone who saw it thought you were threatened."

"Because Jennifer was stalking us. Think how you'd react if someone were following you all the time. It's creepy! Wouldn't you tell her to back off?"

"I would." I studied Leslie. "Is your hesitation because of Hemi's mom? Because if so, she likes you, and—"

"Amanda's great. She'll be a fantastic mother-in-law."

"You're joking, right?" I looked around. "You don't have a camera crew hiding in the woods that's going to jump out and tell me I'm on *Candid Camera*?"

"No. I came alone." Her expression remained stoic. "Hemi doesn't even know I'm here."

Oh boy. "Then if you don't love him, why'd you agree to move here and marry him?"

"Getting married is the next item on my life's agenda. Go to college, become a teacher, graduate, get married, teach for a while, have some kids, and stay home with them until they're all in school. Teach again until retirement."

"You certainly have your life mapped out."

"I'm a planner."

"So you're settling for the guy who happens to be around when you're ready for the next agenda item? Shouldn't you wait to marry a man you'd kill for?"

Someday, I'd try to be a nicer person. But not today.

However, Leslie didn't flinch at my smart-aleck comment. "Amanda and my parents are college friends. They introduced Hemi and me, and in so many ways we're a perfect match. He's kind and sweet in a goofy way. We share the same values. We want kids. We like reading, traveling, going to restaurants—all the things that make for a fun dating relationship."

"Or a friendship."

"Right. And when I found out that you were his friend, I was jealous." She twisted her engagement ring. "The chemistry between the two of you is obvious."

"That's not tru—"

"I know what I witnessed today when I walked in on you—and all the other times we've run into you."

"I don't know what you think you saw, but Hemi and I are just friends, and I'm not interested in getting married right now. I have my own agenda, and that's not part of the plan. Besides, I'm dating someone else."

"Hemi did say something about you wanting to be a journalist in a city—and that you're seeing that hot ufologist who was with you at the restaurant."

"All true statements," I said. "Don't you and Hemi have chemistry?"

"No matter how much we have in common, no matter how much we share the same values, no matter how much he checks every box, there's no spark." She sat up. "Do you think I'm crazy?"

"No. But if you're so upset that you're telling *me* this, then you already know what you have to do."

"Break up with him?"

I decided to remain silent, which was quite an accomplishment.

"I can't." She tucked a strand of hair behind her ear. "I can't let a nice guy go because I don't feel my tummy flutter when we kiss. What if he's my one chance, and I die alone? I'll learn to be in love with him." She hopped up and wagged a finger at me. "Don't you dare tell Hemi any of what I said. Or anyone else."

"I won't."

"Promise?"

"Promise."

She dropped back into her chair. "Or you want Hemi for yourself, and you'll sabotage me."

"I *won't*." I gritted my teeth and tried to process the shifts in this bizarre conversation.

"Good. Hemi's mine, and don't you forget it."

The turmoil in Leslie's eyes was genuine, and I wondered about her sanity. In spite of Hemi's claims to the contrary, *was* she capable of murdering Jennifer? Leslie said she didn't love Hemi enough to kill for him, but was she viewing him as a possession that Jennifer had been threatening to snatch away?

And here I was, sitting alone in my parents' house in the middle of the woods with a woman who was possibly unstable. At least Mom didn't have a knife block sitting out in the kitchen.

Pushing horror movie scenes from my imagination, I stood. "Is there anything else you'd like to discuss before you go?"

Leslie picked a hangnail. "Have you found anything at all that will help me?"

I told her I'd ruled out Scott and Margo Blanchard and had begun focusing on learning more about Jennifer's life. I shared my conversations with Tina Ferguson. "Are you certain that you never left the gym on Saturday morning? Because Tina claims you weren't in there when she went to introduce herself to you."

"I'm telling the truth," Leslie said. "But I went behind the curtain to look for an extension cord for my boom box because Shira Elliot told me there was one back there if I needed it. That must've been when Tina came in."

"Bad timing."

"No kidding. But speaking of Shira, you know how she works at Wildcat Springs Bank and Trust?"

"I've never seen her in there," I said. "She must've just started."

"Well, I went in to cash a check the other day, and I got in line behind Jennifer. She and Shira were whisper arguing—and it sounded personal."

"What about?" Jennifer had worked for Shira's mother Della before she died.

"Jennifer kept saying she didn't want her money, but Shira didn't believe her. Finally, Shira told her to leave because their bank business was done. Jennifer stormed out and didn't even notice me in line behind her."

Could Shira have been assuming that Jennifer was searching for information about Phineas in hopes of earning the reward that Della had once offered to anyone who found the truth? "What'd Shira say when she helped you?"

"She pretended like nothing was wrong, cashed my check, and insisted on giving me a mix tape with the songs she uses in her aerobics class. I have my own music and routines, but she wouldn't take *no* for an answer."

"Did you tell Detective Melchor or Detective Harrell everything you told me?"

"Yes," she said. "But Shira dropped off the tape at Amanda's house on Friday night because she was planning to leave early to go boating at the reservoir with her family early on Saturday, so I doubt she killed Jennifer."

"Saturday night, she came into Chuckie's to order takeout—and she'd definitely spent time in the sun."

Tears welled in Leslie's eyes. "I just know I'm going to jail for something I didn't do."

"Don't give up hope yet." I prayed I sounded more reassuring than I felt, but I knew one thing. I'd be paying Shira Elliot a visit at the bank tomorrow morning.

———

Since Misty'd recovered from her Oreo binge, she gave me a call, and I agreed to meet her at Tate's Place that night. As much as I wanted to tell someone what I'd learned about Leslie and Hemi's relationship, I'd given Leslie my word.

And a promise was a promise.

Still, as I drove into town, I found myself growing more and more irritated with Leslie's attitude. "Doesn't she realize she's robbing Hemi of the opportunity to be with someone who truly loves him? A nice girl who wants to be with him because she's completely in love with him. Leslie's robbing her too. She may not be a murderer, but she's a thief." I squeezed the steering wheel. "Why am I helping a love thief?"

Eduardo Escort had no answer.

This matter was still bugging me when I walked into Tate's Place where Hemi was talking to Kurt at the bar. When I passed, they were engrossed in a conversation about racing go karts, but before I could slip into a corner booth, Kurt looked up and waved, which caused Hemi to whip around.

He jumped off the stool and blocked my path. "Leslie wasn't mad about me asking you to investigate. She thought it was sweet."

"That's good." I knew I should play dumb but lacked motivation to sell the act.

"It is." He rubbed the back of his neck.

"You don't sound relieved," I said. "Why?"

"I'm puzzled, to be honest," he said. "I don't want her to be upset, but I thought she'd have more of an opinion."

I arched an eyebrow. "Because . . . ?"

"Never mind."

Was *he* playing dumb, or was he truly that clueless? Since he was male, either could be true.

I put my hand on my hip. "Let me get this straight. You asked me to help your fiancée and to keep it a secret because you were afraid she'd be mad. But she isn't, and you're upset about it? What's wrong with you?"

"Never mind."

"You already said that."

He glanced at his watch. "I should go. I have an early day tomorrow."

"Why're you getting married?"

He looked at his feet. "It's time I settle down. Leslie wants the same thing."

"Do you realize you're about to pledge your life to a woman you can't even be honest with?"

"I didn't want to add to her worries," he mumbled.

"It's more than that. You're having doubts."

"About her innocence?" He met my eyes. "If that's the case, why would I ask you to investigate?"

"Not that kind of doubts."

"Since you know everything, go ahead. Tell me what I'm thinking."

I stepped closer. "You care about Leslie, and you want the best for her. But no matter how much you try to convince yourself that you want to marry her, deep down, you're not certain. She's sweet. She's pretty. You have a lot in common. But something doesn't feel right. Does it?"

He gazed at me. "You don't know what you're talking about. We worked together a month, and that qualifies you to have an opinion about my life?"

"You don't have to marry someone because that's what your mother wants."

His face reddened. "I *want* to marry Leslie. She doesn't run my life and tell me what to do all the time. She doesn't assume she has me pegged or that I'm incapable of making my own decisions."

"Of course she doesn't. Having an opinion would require her to care."

He flinched. "What's that supposed to mean?"

"Nothing."

"You meant every word. You always do. Did Leslie talk to you?"

Now I couldn't meet *his* gaze.

"Look at me."

I stared at my feet, and he tipped my chin upward.

"What'd she say?" He narrowed his eyes.

"If you're so convinced Leslie talked to me, ask her yourself." The intensity of his gaze was so hypnotic that I was having trouble forming words.

"I meant what I said when I told you I wanted to be friends, but if you're not going to be honest, I don't need you in my life. Don't bother clearing Leslie's name. We'll find the truth without you." He stormed toward the door.

"Not if you don't stop lying to yourselves."

But he didn't look back.

CHAPTER 15

THE NEXT MORNING, I drove to Wildcat Springs Bank and Trust with the intention of cashing a check and talking to Shira Elliot. When I went inside, Shira was the only one working behind the counter—and she was on the phone.

"I was supposed to have breakfast with her this morning, but she didn't show up," Shira whined. "When I went to her house, she wasn't there, and I called the library. She's not working, and her parents haven't heard from her either. I'm telling you, something's wrong." She paused to listen and glanced over at me. "Fine. Thanks for nothing." She slammed the phone down. "Hey, there. You're the waitress from Chuckie's I talked to the other day, right?"

"Yeah." I gave her a sympathetic smile. "It looks like you're having a bad day."

"You could say that again." She removed a tissue from her pocket. "My best friend Tina is missing, and the idiots at the sheriff's department aren't taking me seriously. I've known her for ten years, and she *always* provides too much information. She wouldn't leave town without telling me—especially when we had breakfast plans."

I had to agree with Shira. Tina would've told her best friend where she was going. "Why hasn't her family missed her?"

"Her husband's on a business trip, and their only son's at church camp."

"Maybe she had another emergency, and you'll hear from her soon."

"I hope." Shira sniffled and wiped her sunburned nose. "Now what can I do for you?"

"I need cash, please." I handed her a check. "I hate to ask, but have you heard any more rumors about your uncle Phineas's ghost killing Jennifer Coulter?"

Shira rolled her eyes. "People know better than to say anything to me."

"My grandma mentioned something about how your mother once offered a reward for information about his death. Do people still try for the money?"

"Believe it or not, yes." Shira took bills from her drawer. "Before my mother passed, she convinced Jennifer Coulter to carry on the search for answers. When Jennifer told me about it, I thought she was after money."

"But she wasn't?"

"No. She wanted to honor my mom's memory by finding the truth. Jennifer finally convinced me that if she found the truth, it could end the ghost rumors once and for all." Shira handed me the cash.

"Did Jennifer ever share her theories about what'd happened to Phineas?" I tucked the bills into my wallet.

"No," Shira said. "You don't think her search had something to do with why she died, do you?"

"Possibly."

"I don't know." Shira leaned against the counter. "When Jennifer worked as my mom's caretaker, she was always wonderful to her. But Jennifer's personal life was in constant upheaval. She had one boyfriend after another and never seemed to find anyone who could make her happy. If I were investigating, I'd be looking at the men in her life."

"Do you know who she was involved with recently?"

Shira bent closer. "You didn't hear this from me, but Tina told me she heard a rumor that Jennifer and Scott Blanchard were having an affair, so what if *he* killed her?"

So Tina had known more about Jennifer's personal life than she'd let on. "I heard that too, but Scott was at the parade committee meeting, so he couldn't have. Did you ever see Jennifer with an older, dark-haired man with a mustache?"

"No, and Tina never mentioned that either." She bit her lip. "I'm sorry I can't help you more, but I can't even find my best friend."

I nodded. "I hope Tina's okay." I snatched a strawberry sucker from the basket on the counter and exited the bank as an ambulance wailed past and zoomed into the community center parking lot. Shading my eyes, I stopped on the sidewalk and tried to see what was happening.

Shira rushed outside and stood beside me. "No. What if . . .?" She bolted across the street, and I followed her to the community center's entrance where Scott Blanchard was holding the door open for the paramedics.

"What happened?" Shira demanded.

"When I opened this morning, I found an unconscious woman at the foot of the main staircase," he said. "It looks like she fell."

Shira rushed up the steps, but Scott stepped in front of her, blocking the door. "Please, let the paramedics do their job."

"But my friend is missing!" Shira wailed. "It could be her! Tina's always been such a klutz!"

After watching Tina in aerobics class, I didn't have to stretch my imagination to picture her tumbling down the stairs.

"Did you find the woman's ID?" I asked Scott.

"No, but she looks familiar." He looked away and ran his fingers through his hair. "I-I walked in this morning and found her. I don't even know how she got in because the door was locked."

"Does she have short blonde hair? Blue eyeshadow?" Shira clasped her hands, as if praying for it not to be true.

Scott nodded.

"No!" Shira covered her face with her hands.

"Why don't you wait for the paramedics to bring her out, and if it's Tina, you can follow the ambulance to the hospital," I said.

Shira wrapped her arms around her waist, and I stayed with her until the paramedics rolled a woman on a stretcher out of the building.

Sure enough, the victim was Tina Ferguson.

After the ambulance and Shira were gone, Scott turned to me. "This wasn't how I anticipated starting my day . . . I just hope Tina will be all right."

"Me too," I said. "I'm praying she survives."

I trudged back toward the bank parking lot but stopped when a car parked on the street, and Detectives Melchor and Harrell got out. Scott froze on the steps and stared at the detectives. Tightening my grip on my purse, I remembered the copy of Phineas's letter that I intended to give them.

"What're *you* doing here, Miss Baxter?" Detective Melchor asked, his bald scalp shining in the sun.

"I was at the bank, witnessed the commotion, and came over to see what was happening." I pointed across the street.

"Funny how you're always in the right place at the right time," he said.

"It's a gift." I didn't flinch under his cold gaze.

"Miss Baxter, will you please excuse us while we speak to Mr. Blanchard?" Detective Harrell said.

"Absolutely, but when you're finished, I'd like to speak with you as well." I motioned toward the playground. "I'll wait over there." I strolled to the bench near the swing set, sat where I had a view of Scott and the detectives, and strained to listen.

" . . . opened the door and found her . . . called for help right away."

"Did you know Tina?" Detective Melchor asked.

"I've, uh, seen her at the community center and . . . around town." He ducked his head and shoved his hands into his pockets.

He was definitely hiding something. I stood and moved closer but stopped next to a tree and tried to appear casual.

"Is there something else you'd like to tell us, Mr. Blanchard?" Detective Harrell asked.

"Yes, but first you should know that I was at home with my wife last night!"

The detectives glanced at each other.

Oh boy. This ought to be good.

"Go on," Detective Harrell said.

Scott's shoulders slumped, and he ran his fingers through his hair. "Tina and I went to the same high school near Fort Wayne. Years ago, we ran into each other at a bar and had a fling when she was in the middle of a divorce from her first husband." He scowled. "I wasn't even married yet—and hadn't even met my wife. I've barely talked to Tina since then."

"Yet somehow you both ended up in Wildcat Springs."

"I know how it sounds, but my wife is from Richardville and wanted to open a women's clothing store in her hometown. I thought the job at the community center sounded fun. I lost touch with Tina and didn't know she was living here until I ran into her at the center one day."

"That must've been quite a shock." Detective Melchor smirked.

"No." Scott took a step back. "We were ancient history. Tina dumped me, but honestly, it was pretty obvious we weren't going to work out. I wasn't exactly heartbroken then, and I certainly don't care now. I love my wife."

"Then why'd you hesitate to tell us about your past with Tina?" Detective Harrell asked.

"I knew how it would look." Scott pressed his lips together. "Are we done here?"

"For now," Detective Melchor said.

While Scott plodded into the community center, I approached the detectives and withdrew Nadia's letter to Phineas from my purse.

"What's that, Miss Baxter?" Detective Harrell asked.

I handed her the letter. "Jennifer had this in her possession."

Detective Harrell took the letter and read it while Detective Melchor peered over her shoulder. "How'd you get it?" she asked.

"I had permission to look in Jennifer's desk at the library. This was tucked into a notebook."

"And who allowed you to snoop?" She narrowed her eyes.

"Tina Ferguson."

The detectives exchanged glances.

"Do you think Jennifer stumbled into a secret about Phineas Jones that someone wanted to keep quiet?" I asked. "And that same person thought Tina knew more than she did?"

"I can't comment, Miss Baxter," Detective Harrell said, "but if that *is* the case, for your own safety, I suggest you let *us* conduct the investigation."

Detective Melchor cleared his throat. "And when she says 'suggest,' she means we *expect* you to back off. Got it?"

"Got it."

But as I stomped to my car, I vowed to keep going until I uncovered the truth.

CHAPTER 16

THAT MORNING WHILE I WORKED, I couldn't get Tina off my mind. Why had she been in the community center? Why had she seemed so nervous Saturday—and yesterday? Had she been trying to figure out what'd happened, and someone had tried to silence her? Could Scott Blanchard have found a way to kill Jennifer and attempted to murder Tina too? Or had clumsy Tina taken an accidental tumble?

Flossie Perkins came in for lunch at Chuckie's, and when I went to her table to take her order, she blurted, "Have you heard the ghost of Phineas Jones has struck again and shoved poor Tina Ferguson down the stairs?"

"I'm aware she fell. Have you heard *why* Tina was alone at the community center?"

"Tina is Judy Beeson's great-niece by marriage, and Judy told me Tina was at a sweatshirt decorating class last night. But I have no idea why she stayed in the building after it was over." Flossie smoothed her placemat. "I wish Phineas could have some peace, and then things like this wouldn't happen. He was never a vengeful person in life."

Disagreeing with her about Phineas's ghostly existence would be counterproductive, so I asked, "What do you think is causing Phineas's lack of peace?"

She studied me with her beady eyes. "A broken heart."

She made this statement as if the answer were obvious, but I didn't see how it could be when a ghost was involved. "Last Saturday, you mentioned Phineas carrying a torch for someone. Do you know who?" I hoped it was Nadia.

Flossie stared into space. "Her name was Nadia, and Phineas met her in 1934 when she was an equestrian performer passing through town with the traveling circus."

Equestrian performer? Was Nadia the woman in Grandma's photo album?

"He told me it was love at first sight—at least for him," Flossie continued. "She promised to return but never did. One day her letters stopped, and when Phineas tried to find her, he couldn't."

"Do you think that's why he killed himself?"

"I do, because from what I could see, he never got over her. Such a tragedy." Flossie clicked her tongue and glanced at the menu on her placemat. "I'll have the chicken sandwich basket and black coffee."

———

That afternoon during the daily lull, I took a break and was sipping a Coke when Chuckie waddled out of his office. Doughy and middle-aged, he really was shaped like an avocado.

"You got a phone call, sweetie." He filled a glass with iced tea. "It's your boyfriend, Luke."

"You mean *Duke?*"

"I reckon that's what he said. I need hearing aids." He wedged himself into a booth and guzzled his tea. "I'll stay out here and give you some privacy."

I hurried to Chuckie's office and answered the phone.

"Are you free tonight?" Duke asked.

"Yes." I picked up Chuckie's glass chicken paper weight and examined it. "What's going on?"

"I couldn't wait until Friday to see you."

Ever the smooth talker. "And?" I put the paper weight back.

"I'm coming to Wildcat Springs to poke around at the community center because I might include a chapter about it in my new book about haunted buildings."

With a grin, I sat on the edge of Chuckie's desk. "I see you took my suggestion. But what if there isn't a ghost at the community center?"

"That's why I'm investigating, so I'd love it if you'd join me."

Duke was never boring. "When you say investigating, you mean ghost hunting?"

"That's right," he said. "I've spoken on the phone with a paranormal investigator from Charleston, South Carolina, and he gave me some pointers."

"I'm in." Could a ghost hunt be considered a date? What should I wear? Brushing away the thoughts, I forced myself to refocus on the community center. "Are you aware there was another incident in that building last night?"

"Scott Blanchard warned me when I asked permission to search. Are you afraid of Phineas Jones's ghost hurting us?"

"No, because I'm not convinced that he's haunting the building," I said. "There's something else going on—and human beings are fully responsible. Tina Ferguson, the latest victim, was nervous about something both times I talked to her."

"Do you think she killed Jennifer? Or knows who did?"

"Possibly," I said. "And you'll find this interesting. Before Jennifer died, she was doing research for a novel set in the 1930s. I'm wondering if she used Phineas's life as inspiration." I told Duke about the circus, the letter from Nadia, and how she'd disappeared and never returned to Phineas. "I wish I knew what their secret was."

"Have you had a chance to research the circus?" he asked.

"I'm at work until seven, but I'd been planning to go to the library this evening."

"Since you're joining me tonight, how about I do some digging into the Wheeling Brothers Circus this afternoon?"

"I'd really appreciate it."

"Excellent," he said. "I'll pick you up at eight."

"You look beautiful," Duke said when I answered the door that evening.

"Thank you." I smiled as I locked the house.

Misty might not be impressed by the effort I'd put into my hair, but if Duke thought I looked good, I must be doing something right.

"I didn't know how to dress for a ghost hunt." I rolled up my Guess T-shirt sleeves.

"Jeans are perfect." He gave me an appreciative glance.

We followed the sidewalk around the house to Duke's Grand National. "I'd like to state for the record that I don't think we'll find a ghost," I said.

"I wouldn't be so sure." He opened the passenger door for me. "Scott Blanchard is hoping we don't. He wants to put the haunting rumors to rest." He closed the door and walked around to the driver's side.

"How'd your circus research go?" I asked as soon as he got in.

He started the car, and when "So Emotional" blasted through the speakers, he muted Whitney Houston. "This particular traveling circus didn't last long. It was founded in 1928 by Dane Wheeling and was out of business by the end of 1934. During the summer of 1934, a woman known as the Great and Fearless Nadia performed equestrian stunts."

"The letter Nadia wrote to Phineas referenced a secret she was trying to keep from someone named William and how she had to sneak away to write the letter. I wonder if he was part of the circus too?"

"I don't know, but after the Wheeling Brothers Circus ended, I couldn't find any other references to Nadia—and couldn't even find her last name. It doesn't appear that she joined another circus."

"Since Phineas couldn't find her after the letters stopped," I said. "Maybe Nadia was her stage name."

"I thought the same thing."

"I wouldn't even have considered the circus angle if I hadn't seen the letter Nadia wrote to Phineas. I wonder if Jennifer suspected that Nadia or William killed Phineas and that's why she was researching the circus?"

"Could be."

In the distance, the community center loomed, and the sun was sinking toward the horizon.

"Are you nervous?" Duke asked as we pulled into the parking lot.

"No." My stomach flipped when he parked next to the building.

We got out and climbed the steps leading into the old school while the leaves on a sentinel-like maple rustled, as if warning us to turn back.

My imagination was working overtime—again.

"Ready?" he asked.

"Yep." Goosebumps rose on my arms.

Duke unlocked the door and led us into the lobby. Faint illumination from streetlights streamed into the dark space. We stopped next to Phineas's memorial. When I looked at his picture, a cold chill passed over my body, even though the building was stuffy.

Duke examined the picture. "The infamous Phineas Jones. I hope to meet your spirit this evening, sir."

Wincing at Duke's comment, I turned my back on the photo

but imagined Phineas's eyes following my every move. "Where's the light switch?"

Duke flicked on his flashlight, dug through his bag, and handed me one. "It'll be better if we just use flashlights."

"Where do we begin?" I whispered.

"Why are you whispering?"

"Aren't you supposed to whisper when you're ghost hunting?"

"Any ghosts who dwell here already know we're inside," he said.

"Right."

This had to be the weirdest date I'd ever been on. Or maybe Duke didn't consider this a date since he was conducting business. And why was I worried about that now?

"Let's start in the classroom where Phineas died and work our way down," he said.

"Third floor. Room twelve," I whispered. "Whispering and ghost hunting go together like peanut butter and jelly."

"You're right," he whispered. "It *does* feel more natural." Duke opened his bag, removed his camera, and hung it around his neck. Then, he withdrew a compass with a wrist strap and handed it to me. "Keep an eye on the compass as we move around the building."

I handed him my flashlight while I fastened the compass strap around my wrist. "What am I looking for?"

"Sudden movement of the needle. Shaking. Spinning. Those are indicators of paranormal activity. I couldn't get my hands on an EMF reader, but the ghost hunter told me a compass works just as well."

The needle was pointing northwest.

Duke returned my flashlight, and when we stepped onto the creaky stairs, our footsteps echoed through the lobby. I wanted to grab his arm, but since I didn't want to seem like a chicken, I watched the compass, clutched the banister, and softly hummed the *Ghostbusters* song.

Duke joined in as we passed the second floor and crept to the third. The compass moved naturally with our turns, and the temperature rose while the air grew stagnant.

"This is it." Duke stopped at the door to classroom twelve, pushed open the door, and we eased inside.

Nothing had changed since Scott had shown me the room a few days earlier. Student desks were stacked, and the teacher's desk was pushed against the wall.

"Now what?" I brushed a dribble of sweat from my temple.

"We ask Phineas to reveal himself."

"Seriously?"

"It's what the ghost hunter said to do."

Now that I was here, I wasn't certain what God—or Grandma —would say about this adventure. Was I dabbling in something best left alone? But I didn't want Duke to think I was a stick in the mud, and I *was* a journalist pursuing truth. And the truth was, we needed to put ghostly rumors to rest and find out what happened to Jennifer and Tina.

"Okay," I said. "You talked to the expert."

Duke pointed to the teacher's brass bell sitting on a dusty shelf next to a globe. "Phineas Jones, if you're here, ring the bell."

Duke grasped my hand. Eerie silence invaded the room, and I kept my eyes on the compass.

Seconds passed.

Nothing.

I looked at Duke and shrugged.

"You try," Duke said. "He might respond to a woman's voice."

"Phineas Jones, if you're here, will you *please* show us by ringing the teacher's bell?" I tried to sound sweet, which wasn't exactly my baseline.

"You were much more polite than me," he whispered into my ear. "If I were a ghost, that would get me out of hiding." For a second, I thought he was going to kiss me, but he must've realized that would be strange timing, so he stepped back.

We waited. The compass needle held steady, and seconds ticked away. And the longer we stood in the classroom, the more ridiculous I felt. "Maybe he doesn't like bells."

"Good point," he said. "Phineas, please tap the wall."

Sweat dribbled down my back.

And still, there were no sounds—and no drafts of cold air, which wouldn't feel too bad in the stifling classroom.

"Phineas, we're going to walk around the building, and if you'd like to reveal yourself, could you knock on something in the rooms we visit?" Duke asked.

"Please?" I added. "Or if you'd rather, slam a door to vent your anger about Nadia."

We lingered for a minute before creeping to the classroom across the hall.

"We don't need to tiptoe any more than we need to whisper." Duke peeked into the room then stepped aside to let me enter. "But we're both doing it."

This classroom contained more stacked desks, and a white sheet was draped over the teacher's desk. We stood in the middle of the room and waited.

"Phineas?"

Silence.

We made our way through the classrooms, the gym, the library, and the cafeteria. But the compass behaved normally, and the only sounds were our footsteps, our breathing, and intermittent sounds of passing cars outside.

"We haven't checked the basement," Duke said as we returned to the lobby.

"The custodial closet is next to the boiler room. His ghost might like to hang out there." We descended the basement stairs and entered the men's locker room. When we didn't find anything, we checked the women's locker room.

I stopped and pointed at the bench. "I found Jennifer here."

"That's such a shame," Duke said. "She had her whole life ahead of her."

"I know." One more reason to keep digging for the truth.

"Phineas, will you reveal yourself?" Duke paused next to the sinks.

We waited.

"This is absurd," I mumbled.

"We have to be thorough." He held the door for me, and we edged to the end of the hallway where the boiler room beckoned.

"This is the creepiest room in the entire building." I opened a closet, and a wave of mildewy air assaulted my nose. A mop and bucket were propped against a shelf of cleaning supplies.

A small office was on our left, and we entered. Something crunched under my foot, and when I bent down, a crushed red brick chip lay on the concrete. I glanced around at the white-washed brick walls for signs of crumbling, but they appeared to be intact. A pocked bulletin board hug above a desk and chair with duct tape holding the padding together. Three dented gray lockers were pushed against the far wall. I leaned against the desk.

"Call for him again," Duke said.

"Phineas, please rap on the lockers. Or whatever you want. At this point, you could warble Sinatra for all I care."

Duke chuckled. "'Strangers in the Night'?"

"'My Way'?"

"'I'm Walking Behind You'?"

"'Somethin' Stupid'?" I put a hand on my hip.

Duke's eyes glimmered. "'Let Me Try Again'?"

"'I'm a Fool to Want You.'"

"'The Best is Yet to Come,'" we said in unison.

We waited, and I kept my eyes on the compass needle that held steady. "We've been everywhere in the building and haven't seen or heard anything. Does this mean we've proven it isn't haunted?"

Duke looked around. "It doesn't appear to be now, but that doesn't mean it wasn't at one time."

I glanced at the compass again, but this time, out of the corner of my eye, I noticed an arc etched into the concrete floor next to the locker bank. I focused my beam on it. "Look. The floors are scratched—like the lockers have been moved away from the wall."

Duke studied the locker bank. "They aren't sitting square against the wall either, but maybe it's because the wall is bowing." He handed me his flashlight, and metal screeched against concrete when he dragged the lockers in the direction of the arc, revealing a manhole cover on the floor underneath.

CHAPTER 17

DUKE and I exchanged glances before he opened the manhole cover. While I shone my flashlight into the opening, he took pictures. A metal ladder led into a tunnel.

"Do we check out what's down there?" I asked.

"I'm game." Duke let his camera hang around his neck and descended into the hole. The space at the bottom was large enough for him to walk upright. "Are you coming?"

"Duh. I'm not staying by myself in the creepy boiler room." I gripped the metal rungs and lowered myself into the musty depths. When I reached the bottom, the walls and floor were red brick, and a few of them appeared crumbly. "Someone must've been here recently and tracked that brick chip that I stepped on upstairs."

"Makes sense." Duke moved his flashlight around.

"Did Scott mention anything about the tunnel when you asked permission to search?"

"Not a word, so I wonder if he even knows about it."

"How long do you think it's been here?" I had a sudden image of bootleggers running moonshine through the tunnels and stifled a chuckle at the stray thought.

Duke aimed his flashlight onto a pipe running along the ceiling. "My guess is since the school was built because it's a maintenance tunnel." He grinned. "Want to see where it leads?"

"Obviously." I rubbed my arms because of the damp, chilly air shrouding us.

"Right or left first?"

"Left."

We inched through the narrow passageway, taking care not to trip on the buckled floor. According to the compass, we were walking south, which meant the tunnel's path was leading us under the building and was running parallel to several pipes.

More importantly, the compass needle wasn't detecting ghostly activity.

The tunnel forced us to the left and revealed more pipes, brick walls, and floors.

"There's another ladder ahead," he said as we hurried toward a dead end.

He put his flashlight into his mouth, grasped the rungs, and climbed the ladder. When he reached the top, a click echoed through the tunnel.

"I'm trying to get the hatch open." He pounded his fist against the door, and when it flew open, he stuck his head through. "Oh wow. Come on up."

He disappeared, and I didn't waste any time climbing the ladder. When I reached the top, I realized what had caused Duke's reaction—a narrow room with a staircase and an old-fashioned, porcelain drinking fountain.

"It looks like they sealed off this section." He concentrated his flashlight beam on the space.

I pointed to the brick wall. "You're right. I'd have to ask my grandma, but years ago, there was a fire, and I know they demolished part of the building and used the space that wasn't damaged."

Duke climbed the stairs, and I followed him into another area nearly identical to the floor below. We proceeded to the third floor where the space felt bigger because the stairs ended, and we found ourselves in a room about ten feet wide. I moved in a slow circle, taking in the room that felt like a time capsule.

"Someone moving around in the tunnels and the sealed area would explain the noises that Flossie Perkins reported," he said.

"Surely, she knew about part of the building being sealed," I said. "I wonder why no one ever thought to look in the tunnels to put the ghost rumors to rest."

"That's a good question." Duke descended the stairs, and gritting my teeth, I followed him back into the tunnel. It guided us away from the building to a dead end where another ladder led to another ceiling hatch.

He climbed up, pushed, and the door flew open. A cool breeze flowed toward me as Duke popped through the opening before ducking back down.

"It's safe."

He disappeared, and I followed him outside into a small clearing in the middle of the woods behind the school. We stood beside the open cover and looked around.

"If I were trying to sneak into the school, I'd use this access point," I said. "Plenty of trees mean you could get in and out undetected."

"Except, you'd have to have a key." He shined his flashlight on the keyhole. "I'd be interested to see what Detectives Melchor and Harrell have to say, considering a murder and a suspicious accident just happened in the building."

We descended into the tunnel, and this time we walked more quickly. When we arrived back at the community center basement, Duke replaced the locker bank. We hurried outside, and he locked the front door.

"Are you disappointed we didn't find a ghost?" I asked.

"Not at all. I find the paranormal fascinating, but an old maintenance tunnel and sealed-off stairwell are much more intriguing."

———

The next morning, I got up early and went to Della's Donuts with the intention of buying two of Grandma's favorite cinnamon-coated donuts. A line was snaking outside the door when I arrived, but this didn't deter me, so I took my place behind a man in a fishing vest and hat.

The line moved quickly, and before long, I was inside the shop that Shira Elliot's mother had owned when she was alive. When the new owners had purchased the business, they'd kept the name to honor Della Jones-Nash. They'd saved the framed photos that documented the shop's history. They showed Della working behind the counter and in the kitchen, but until today, I'd never paid attention to the other folks.

According to the pictures, Phineas had worked in his sister's shop. He and another man who looked vaguely familiar were cutting out and frying donuts in one of the pictures. Because Phineas looked younger than he did in the school's memorial picture, I guessed he worked here before becoming a custodian. I squinted at the photo. Who was that man with Phineas?

I tapped the fisherman in front of me on the shoulder. "Excuse me, sir?"

He turned around. "Morning, miss."

"Have you been a long-time resident of Wildcat Springs?"

"That's a polite way of asking if I'm old, ain't it?" He guffawed. "But, yes, I've lived here for all of my seventy-seven years."

I pointed at the photo of Phineas and the other man. "Do you recognize the man who's in this photo with Phineas Jones? He looks familiar, but I can't place him."

"That there is Vernon Wise. He and Phineas were buddies, and they used to help Della in the shop every so often. At least until Phin went and hanged himself." He shook his head. "Such a shame."

"Does Vernon still live in town?"

"He lives in that ramshackle house over by the old school." He chuckled. "Could be why Phin haunts the place. Wants to be near his old pal."

"I know the house. The one with the barking dog." *And his creepy, overall-wearing owner.*

"Arrow always sounds like he'll take your leg off, but he's a friendly little fella once he recognizes you. Same with Vernon."

While he placed his order, I added Vernon Wise to the list of things I needed to discuss with Grandma. After purchasing my donuts, I drove to her house.

I wasn't worried about her being awake because she believed staying in bed after six was sinful. Sure enough, I found her weeding around the green beans in her vegetable garden.

"What's wrong?" She rose to her feet and stripped off her gloves.

"Why does something have to be wrong? I thought you'd be glad to see me."

She glanced at her watch. "At seven-thirty? I didn't know you were capable of getting out of bed before eight."

"I brought your favorite donuts." I displayed the sack.

"You want something and don't care if your old grandma gets diabetes."

"Your blood sugar is fine. I overheard Mom say she was jealous of your numbers."

"My cholesterol then. Now what do you want?"

"To thank you again for fixing my tires. It's nice to have Eduardo Escort back."

"You're welcome." She brushed her hands, snatched the sack, and peeked inside. "Want some milk?"

"Yes, please."

She pointed at one of the rocking chairs on her back porch. "Have a seat. I'll be back, and you can tell me why you're really here." She plunked the donuts onto the table between the chairs and hustled inside.

A few minutes later, she returned with the milk and settled into her rocking chair.

I let her eat a few bites before I proceeded. "Do you know anything about Vernon Wise?"

"The old coot that lives next to the school?"

"Yeah."

"Not much." She pinched off a donut piece. "A couple of weeks ago, we got a prayer chain request for him because his cousin goes to our church. Vernon's got lung cancer."

"What's the prognosis?"

"I don't know. Probably not good since he's a chain smoker." She rocked back and forth. "You got up at the crack of dawn to come ask me about Vernon Wise?"

"No." I told her what I'd seen at the donut shop. "Actually, I wanted to ask if you knew about the maintenance tunnel that runs under the old Wildcat Springs school since you and Grandpa went there."

"Nope." She shook her head. "I'm guessing that was something they didn't want students to know about."

"And did you go to school there before or after they sealed off the staircase?"

"During. There was a fire that destroyed the old kitchen and cafeteria, and when the crew did repairs, they relocated the kitchen and cafeteria and sealed off some of the building that'd survived the fire."

"Did any students ever try to get into the sealed-off area?"

"I didn't know that was possible," she said. "As far as the students knew, the area was secured, although, I suppose that's what they told us so some ornery boys wouldn't take it upon themselves to go on a mission. I never heard about anyone trying, though. How'd you hear about it?"

I told her what Duke and I had discovered the night before, but when she stopped eating her donut, I knew I was in trouble.

"Let me see if I understand," she said. "You went ghost hunting with a man you barely know, and who led you into the maintenance tunnel of a one-hundred-year-old building that should've been demolished instead of being made into the community center. Does that sum it up?"

"Yes."

She compressed her lips. "You're not just lacking common sense. You're a complete moron."

I was used to Grandma's name calling, but I did want clarification. "Why?"

"God-fearing girls don't go ghost hunting."

"They do when they're pursuing truth," I said. "And we proved once and for all the old school isn't haunted. If it makes you feel better, I wondered how God would feel about it."

"It doesn't," she snapped. "You were alone with a strange man in a dark building at night. Do you want people to think you're a tramp?"

"I thought you wanted me to find a man who'll get me pregnant."

"Not before you're married, young lady."

"Nothing happened," I said. "Besides, Duke isn't a stranger to *me*."

"*I've* never met him, but I don't suppose it occurred to you to introduce him to your old grandma. Have your parents met him?"

"Just Dad."

"Mmhmm. Rochelle?"

"No."

"He's coming to dinner. Tonight." She folded her arms. "Call him and tell him—"

"But what if he's—?"

"Busy? If he values you, he won't be. He'll be thrilled to meet your grandma."

"I thought you'd be happy I have a man interested in me."

"I need to meet him before I decide how I feel." She resumed eating, and then said, "But I'm proud of you."

I nearly choked. "What? *Why?*"

"You may be a moron, but you're a moron with moxie."

CHAPTER 18

LATER THAT MORNING, I decided to attend Jennifer Coulter's funeral with Rochelle. I was hoping the mystery man with the Magnum P.I. mustache would come to pay his respects.

"I don't understand why you're putting yourself through this," Rochelle said as soon as I got into her blue Chevette. "You hardly knew Jennifer."

"But I talked to her the night before she died *and* invited her to the aerobics class. I feel responsible."

"You shouldn't. It was her time." She exited Mom and Dad's driveway and sped along the winding road leading through Wildcat Woods. "But you're still trying to figure out what happened, aren't you?"

"Yes." There wasn't any point in hiding the truth.

Rochelle sighed. "You're not going to embarrass me by asking her family a bunch of questions, are you? They're grieving."

"I'm going to observe behavior—and watch who's there to mourn."

"That'd better be *all* you do." She reached over, cranked up the radio, and sang along with Billy Ocean.

When we arrived at the funeral home, the room was packed, so we found seats in the back row. I scanned the crowd and recognized Jennifer's brother Monty and her parents. Flossie Perkins was a few rows in front of us.

But I didn't see the man from Jennifer's photo.

When Monty saw me, he waved, hopped up, and hurried over. He was wearing cowboy boots and a white shirt with a turquoise bolo tie. I'd never noticed until today, but his eyes were the same green as his sister's.

I stood and hugged him. "I'm sorry about Jennifer."

He swallowed and glanced at his watch. "We have a few minutes before the service. Could we talk in private?"

"Sure."

Rochelle pressed her lips together, but she shouldn't have disapproved because I hadn't sought Monty out.

He led me out into a hallway with floral wallpaper. We passed the restrooms, and I hoped we wouldn't go any deeper into the funeral home's bowels and accidentally stumble into the embalming room.

Finally, he stopped near an emergency exit and pay phone. "I heard you're studying to be a reporter and have been trying to figure out what happened to Jen."

"I just want to find the truth."

"All the crap people are saying about my sister isn't true."

"Such as?"

"First off, she wasn't trying to steal Hemi from his fiancée. She wanted to apologize for how she'd treated him in high school."

"Is that why she wrote a letter to Hemi with all of the memories about their good times?"

He fiddled with his tie. "She had me read it, and there was nothing inappropriate. She was reminiscing and wanted to get together to apologize in person."

"But Leslie didn't take it that way." I wished she hadn't destroyed it so I could judge for myself.

"Right."

"What about all the times Hemi and Leslie ran into Jennifer?" I asked. "Leslie felt as if she were being stalked."

"Coincidence?" Monty shrugged. "We live in a small town. Since Jennifer worked here too, she did a lot of her business in Wildcat Springs."

His explanation made sense. "Had Jennifer told your family she was pregnant?" Inwardly, I winced at my question's boldness, but to my surprise, Monty didn't flinch.

"Yeah—the day before she died."

"How'd everyone react?" I asked.

"My parents would've preferred that she be married first, but they weren't upset—they actually seemed excited about having their first grandchild. I wished she had a husband to help her raise the baby, but I was looking forward to having a niece or nephew." His Adam's apple bobbed.

Since Monty didn't appear to mind my questions, I decided to continue. "Do you think the baby's father might've killed her?"

"I've been asking myself that." Monty leaned against the wall. "Jennifer told us she went to a sperm bank and was artificially inseminated, but we found that hard to believe because it's expensive. She didn't have extra money, and none of us loaned her any. *I* think she was seeing a married guy, and she was protecting him."

"But you don't know who she was seeing?"

"No, and believe me, if I did, I'd be pounding on his door to ask a few questions." He curled his fingers into a fist.

Could Scott Blanchard have killed Jennifer *before* his meeting on Saturday morning and paid Tina and Vernon to lie about seeing her at 9:35? What if Tina, because of her financial problems, had demanded more money, and Scott had pushed her?

Organ music played, signaling the service was about to begin, so Monty and I walked down the hall. Just then, the mystery man with the mustache entered, so I nudged Monty. "Can you remind me who that man is? He looks familiar, but I can't place him."

"That's my uncle John. He doesn't have any kids, so he's

always treated Jen and me like we were his own. Jen's death has hit him hard."

"Is it possible Jennifer borrowed money from your uncle?" I whispered.

"Definitely not. He got into financial trouble years ago—made some bad investments—and is still trying to dig himself out of the hole by working two jobs. He barely has enough extra to give birthday and Christmas gifts, but we always get a little something from him." Monty paused next to the entry. "I'd better get back in there."

"One more thing." I rested my hand on his arm. "Did Jennifer ever talk about the novel she was writing?"

"A novel?" He blinked. "She wasn't writing a novel."

"Are you sure? Because one of her coworkers mentioned Jennifer doing research for a mystery novel about a circus."

He snorted. "Then either the coworker or my sister was lying because she wasn't the type to write a book."

After Jennifer's funeral, I had to work, but before I left, I took Grandma's photo album from my bookshelf and opened it to the circus pictures. I sat on my bed and gently slipped the picture of Nadia sitting on a horse from the album to take a closer look, but it wasn't a photo.

It was a souvenir postcard.

No one had written on the card, but the label on the back read, *The Great and Fearless Nadia Allen performs for the Wheeling Brothers Circus*.

Something about her name seemed vaguely familiar, but I couldn't figure out why. I put the postcard into the album and examined the other circus picture of the man on stilts. It was also a postcard, and the man's name was William Allen. Was he Nadia's brother? He didn't appear old enough to be her father, and if that were the case, she wouldn't have referred to him by his first name in the letter. A stepfather would've had a different last name. If he were an uncle, it was likely that she would've used the title with his name. I removed the copy of Phineas's letter from my purse and re-read Nadia's words.

William is keeping a close eye on me, and I had to sneak away to write this letter. Please don't write back because he must never know the secret with which I have entrusted you. It is my only hope of having my freedom someday.

Had William disapproved of her relationship with Phineas? What was the secret Nadia had referenced? And why did she feel the need to be free?

I secured the postcard in the album and returned it to my shelf. Now that I had some last names, I'd do some more digging —as soon as possible.

CHAPTER 19

"I FEEL terrible about the short notice," I told Duke that evening as he drove to Grandma's house in Wildcat Springs.

"Don't. I'm thrilled to meet your grandma." He reached over and clasped my hand.

"When dinner is over, I'm going to remind you that you said that."

"Because of the food?"

"Grandma's a little hit and miss in the kitchen, but I wasn't thinking about the food."

"Personality?"

"Something like that."

"I'm intrigued." He parked on the street in front of Grandma's house, and when we got out of the car, he opened the trunk and withdrew a bottle of wine.

"What're you doing?" I froze.

"I have a hostess gift. This is a fine—"

"No way." I shook my head and fought back the urge to bat the bottle out of his hand. "Grandma doesn't drink."

"Ever?"

"She's never had alcohol pass through her lips." I looked up at the house and prayed she wasn't spying at the window.

He put the bottle back in the trunk. "I'm afraid I don't have an alternative gift."

I slammed the trunk. "No gift is better than the wrong gift."

"I suppose," he said as we walked toward the porch. "How does she feel about you frequenting Tate's Place?"

"She doesn't know, so let's keep it that way." Cringing at the thought of her finding out, I rang the doorbell.

"My lips are sealed."

The door swung open, and Grandma answered, wearing a lavender sundress with a yellow apron.

"Hmph." She popped a hand onto her hip and scrutinized Duke. "You're too handsome for your own good."

He winced. "Thank—"

"How old are you? You've got at least a decade on my granddaughter, unless you're not aging well, and if so, that's too bad. Although, men look more distinguished as they age, so that's working in your favor."

Duke opened his mouth, snapped it shut, and said, "I'm thirty-two."

"I've always been a good judge of age," Grandma said. "I'm seventy-two, if you're wondering."

"I wouldn't have guessed you were more than sixty-three," he said.

"Aren't you a smooth operator?"

"You honestly don't look like a septuagenarian."

"Thank you, but as I tell Bobbi Sue all the time, no one likes a show-off who uses fancy words."

He glanced at me. "I'm—"

"Now that we know everybody's age, are we allowed inside?" I grasped Duke's bicep, in part, because I thought there was a decent chance that he was about to bounce.

"Well, I reckon I ought to make sure supper's not burning." She stepped aside and marched to the kitchen.

I sniffed the air and determined we were having fried chicken.

"How are you holding up?" I whispered as I locked the front door. "That was just the opening round."

Duke glanced at the dead bolt. "Does she know we've only been on a few dates? Because I'm getting the feeling she thinks I'm here to ask for your hand in marriage."

"She does this with every man I've ever dated, and all of them are alive and well."

"Good to know." His gaze traveled to the couch, and he pointed at the fabric protector. "That can't be comfortable."

"It's not, but it's been there as long as I can remember."

"And well before that." He sat and ran his hand over the plastic.

"Bobbi Sue!" Grandma yelled. "Come stir the gravy while I mash the potatoes. I don't have three hands, you know."

I led Duke into the kitchen.

"Is there something I can do to help, Mrs. Spearman?" he asked.

Grandma turned from the stove. "Call me Isadora. Now what's your name again? I should've had this information considering my granddaughter lost her head and went ghost hunting with you alone at night with absolutely no regard for her reputation—or her family's good name."

"I'm Duke Talbert, and I promise you nothing occurred to damage your granddaughter's reputation."

"You'd better be telling the truth." She shook a beater at him before jamming it into her mixer. "How do you earn a living?"

"I'm an investigative journalist."

"Does it pay well?"

"I didn't go into journalism to get rich."

She shoved in the other beater. "That's a no."

"Duke wrote a book." I stirred the lumpy gravy. "*Close Encounters in the USA.*"

"Did it make the New York Times Bestseller list?"

"No," he said. "But I've already earned out my advance against royalties."

"Hmph." She poured some milk into the potatoes, switched on the mixer, and shouted, "Where'd you grow up?"

"Westfield, Indiana."

"How'd you get into ghost hunting?"

I held my breath and silently prayed Duke wouldn't blame me for his new endeavor.

"I'm writing a book on haunted buildings and decided to investigate the community center in Wildcat Springs. But as far as I could tell, there's no paranormal activity in that old school. Since we discovered the maintenance tunnels and the sealed staircase, I think the strange noises and drafts could be traced back to people accessing the tunnel."

"And because there's no such thing as ghosts." She shut off the mixer and tapped the beaters against the bowl.

"No, because in this instance, it's the most likely explanation."

"You ever been married?" Grandma tossed the beaters into the sink. "Men who look like you don't spend much time off the market."

Thankful Grandma had moved on from the ghost topic, I turned off the burner and poured the gravy into a boat. I should've known the answer to her question—but I didn't.

He cleared his throat. "My divorce was finalized a couple of months ago."

Why had he not told me? How long would it have taken him to share that information if Grandma hadn't been interrogating him?

"So my granddaughter is your rebound?" She took the pot directly to the table, slapped it onto a hot pad, and plunked a serving spoon into the potatoes.

"We've been enjoying each other's company," I said quickly. "I don't think we're serious enough to worry about me being a rebound." I put the gravy on the table.

"Bobbi Sue's right. She's also fun to be with and a breath of fresh air." He grinned at me, and my heart fluttered.

"Why'd you get divorced?" She pointed at the green beans simmering on the stove. "Take those to the table for me."

Duke's eyes clouded as he lifted the pot and carried it to the table. "My ex-wife left me for my former best friend."

"Ouch." Grandma picked up the chicken platter. "That was stupid of her. I'm willing to bet he's nowhere near as good looking as you."

"Thank you, but I should've been more attentive. She didn't like my traveling for work."

"Any kids?" she asked.

"No."

"That's a blessing. Divorce is difficult for little ones." She pointed to a chair. "Duke there. Bobbi Sue next to me." As soon as we were seated, she blessed the food, and after we passed the unintentionally extra-crispy chicken, she said, "I reckon you wonder why I'm being so hard on you."

"The thought crossed my mind," Duke said.

"Has Bobbi Sue told you about her parents' situation?"

"I'm aware they recently left town, and you don't know where they went or how long they'll be gone."

Grandma dropped a heaping spoonful of mashed potatoes onto her plate. "And since her father isn't here to evaluate the men in her life, that job falls to me."

"He'd approve of your efforts."

"Of course he would. Guy and Nicki were going to let my husband and me raise the girls if something happened to them."

He picked up a forkful of limp green beans. "They'd appreciate that you take the job seriously."

"Someone needs to watch out for Bobbi Sue," she said. "I don't worry about Rochelle as much because she's got a husband, and she's never had Bobbi Sue's nose for trouble. I nearly had a heart attack when I got home from my cruise and learned she'd gotten wrapped up in a murder investigation." She doused her mashed potatoes with gravy. "But my being in town doesn't seem to make a difference one way or another. She went and got herself involved in Jennifer Coulter's death investigation, but you probably already know that."

"Have you found any new information?" Duke asked me.

"I took a second look at Grandma's circus photos, which are actually postcards."

"That's right," she said. "I'd forgotten about that."

"Nadia's last name was *Allen,* and the other postcard in the album had a picture of a man named William Allen. I'm thinking he might be her brother." I told them about Phineas's letter. "I wonder what secret she and Phineas were keeping from William."

"That could be the key to understanding what happened to Phineas," Duke said. "Anything else?"

I recapped what I'd learned from Monty at the funeral that morning. "Since Jennifer's brother had no clue that she was writing a novel, I'm wondering if she was using novel research as a cover for poking into Phineas's life and death."

"Why would she need to do that?" Grandma asked.

"If Phineas didn't commit suicide, and people found out Jennifer was looking for the truth, she might've been afraid his killer would come after her," Duke said.

"Sounds like you both need to mind your own beeswax."

I tuned out Grandma as a stray thought sidetracked me. "Wait a second." I set my fork on my plate. "Jennifer's duffel bag was missing."

"What's that got to do with anything?" Grandma asked.

"I know. It sounds weird, but hear me out," I said. "All this time, I've been assuming Jennifer went into the locker room to change for a morning aerobics class, but why wouldn't she wear her workout clothes from home? Why use a grody locker room? Tina reported seeing Jennifer with a duffel bag, but when I found her, there was no bag."

"Because the killer stole it," Duke said.

"Right. Maybe Jennifer wasn't planning to attend aerobics class and was there to snoop in the building. The bag might've contained a critical piece of evidence having to do with Phineas— or her investigation into his death. So the killer took it."

"Makes sense." Duke nodded.

"Not a bad theory," Grandma said.

"I've been feeling guilty since I invited her the night before at—"

Duke tapped my foot under the table.

"Where'd you see Jennifer the night before?" Grandma asked.

Uh-oh. "When I was out and about." I twisted the napkin on my lap.

"In Wildcat Springs?"

"Uh-huh."

"On a Friday night?"

"Yep."

"Isadora, this fried chicken is magnificent," Duke said.

"Young man, it's burned to a crisp, and we all know it." Grandma didn't even look at Duke but directed her glare at me. "Young lady, were you at Tate's Place?"

"I was only drinking Coke."

"In an unwholesome atmosphere."

"I was with friends, and it's not the den of iniquity you're imagining."

She pursed her lips. "It's nice to know you don't care one iota about how your reputation affects your grandmother." She resumed eating mashed potatoes with an offended air.

I grabbed a drumstick, took a bite, and resisted the urge to laugh at Grandma's dramatics. Duke was chasing a stray green bean around his plate as if he were afraid to leave a trace of food, and I had to commend his instincts. When Rochelle and I didn't clean our plates, Grandma still reminded us about the world's starving children.

I had no reason to believe Duke would escape her admonitions.

"Your train of thought about the duffel bag is intriguing, Bobbi Sue," Duke said after he stabbed the wayward green bean with his fork. "And if you're correct, it's possible Jennifer found information about Phineas that someone wanted to keep quiet."

"Grandma, when you spoke with Jennifer at the salon, did she give any indication that she was searching for information about Phineas?"

"*Now* you want my input?"

"You're so upset that I went to a bar with friends and drank a Coke that you're refusing to share evidence that might help us find Jennifer's killer?"

"Why is finding answers up to you?" Grandma rested her fork on her plate.

"You told me Detective Girly Hands Melchor isn't capable."

"But Detective Harrell is an excellent detective, so you don't need to put yourself in danger."

Duke looked back and forth between Grandma and me.

"Could you at least answer one more question, and then we'll talk about something else?" I asked.

"I reckon."

"When Jennifer bought your camera, did she tell you *why* she needed a new one?"

"The same reason everyone needs a new camera." She snorted. "Duke, college isn't making her smarter."

I shoved a forkful of mashed potatoes into my mouth.

"Bobbi Sue was hoping Jennifer mentioned a specific reason, such as research." He nudged my foot.

"She didn't say anything to me about research or anything else for that matter," Grandma said. "Enough about Jennifer and this whole mess. Duke, how many children do you want?"

CHAPTER 20

"I'M SO, SO SORRY," I said as Duke drove me home from Grandma's. "I'm used to Grandma interrogating the men I date, but you're the first person she's ever asked about children."

My face burned as I replayed the scene in my head. Duke had smiled and answered Grandma, but he hadn't disguised the sheer terror in his eyes.

"What an honor." He glanced in the rearview mirror. "I don't think she was happy with my answer, but I've always thought two is a nice number."

"You could've told her you wanted a dozen kids, and it wouldn't be good enough," I muttered.

"I didn't think your question about Jennifer's camera was dumb, by the way."

"I didn't either." I fiddled with the seatbelt. "When Misty and I searched Jennifer's apartment, I didn't find her camera."

"Because it was in her stolen duffel bag?"

"That could be." I thought of the packet of Christmas and Easter pictures that'd been in her apartment and had an idea. "But we might catch a break if Jennifer dropped off film to be developed before she died."

"And didn't have a chance to pick up the pictures?" He stopped at the intersection in Venlap, the tiny burg near my parents' house.

"Exactly," I said. "It may be a long shot, but I'll check the Wildcat Springs drugstore first thing tomorrow morning."

"And I'll do some digging and see if I can find any more information about William and Nadia Allen."

One advantage of living in a small town was that people were trusting—although with the current homicide rate for the year, I was wondering if that was a position we should reevaluate. The good part of this trust was that our developed photos waited in alphabetized baskets unguarded by any of the employees at Otto's Drugs.

I strolled into the store, snagged a shopping basket, and wandered through the makeup aisle. I picked a bottle of dusty rose nail polish and a new tube of mascara before making my way to the photo shelves.

I wouldn't look too suspicious since the picture envelopes with last names beginning with A's, B's and C's were in the same blue plastic bin. I flicked through the stack. When I came upon an envelope labeled *Jennifer Coulter*, I suppressed a squeal.

Shifting casually, I made sure no one was looking before I slipped the stack of photos out of the envelope. The first group of pictures appeared to be from a party, and her parents, uncle, and Monty appeared in several of the photos with groups of people sitting in lawn chairs and eating from paper plates. I recognized some faces from Jennifer's funeral.

But when I was about a third of the way through the stack, I stifled a gasp. Jennifer had found the maintenance tunnel entrance in the school. There was a picture of the lockers shoved aside and the manhole cover.

The next picture was of the tunnel itself, and the pictures that followed included more of the same. Jennifer had taken the same path Duke and I had walked, and she'd even discovered the sealed staircase. Had Jennifer followed the tunnel in the opposite direction? There were no photos of the outside entrance. I counted twenty-four photos. Then, I double checked for another envelope but didn't see one.

What if she'd started a new roll but hadn't had time to finish it?

Had Jennifer told someone about the tunnel? When had she accessed it? Had she been trying to sneak back in that morning, and someone discovered her? But why would someone want to stop her from going into a tunnel so much they'd be willing to kill?

I slipped the pictures into my shopping basket and approached the checkout where a teenage girl was filing her nails. She wouldn't pay enough attention to know if I was Jennifer Coulter or not, so I might as well buy them and give them to Detective Harrell. Maybe she and Detective Melchor had figured out something I hadn't.

"What made you think to check the drugstore for Jennifer's photos?" Detective Harrell asked as we sat at a table in the interrogation room at the sheriff's department.

I'd made a quick trip so I could give her the pictures. "My grandma mentioned that Jennifer had recently purchased an old camera from her, so I wondered if she dropped off film before she died."

"Uh-huh. And that hunch happened to be right."

"It did." I glanced at the one-way glass window and wondered if Detective Melchor was watching me from the other side.

She shook her head. "There's more that you're not telling me, but considering you're trying to help, I'm not going to worry about it."

"How's the investigation coming?" I asked.

"We're making progress."

"Should we expect an arrest soon?"

"I can't comment on an ongoing investigation."

"I suppose you can't tell me if you found Jennifer's camera at the scene? It has a blue and white woven strap. An eyewitnesses saw Jennifer walk into the community center with a bag, but when I found Jennifer, there wasn't a bag."

"And you think someone stole her bag—for the camera?"

"Yes."

"Why?" Her tone didn't hold a bit of doubt—only curiosity—as if she wanted to see what I'd volunteer.

"Because Jennifer may've taken more pictures of the tunnel, but I didn't find another envelope at the store."

"Why do you believe the tunnel is significant?"

"I don't know. Is it possible Jennifer was about to expose the truth about Phineas's death?"

She nodded. "You've certainly given us another angle to pursue, though we were aware that proving Phineas didn't die from suicide was important to Jennifer."

"Do you truly believe Leslie Enright is guilty? Because it's more likely that she was in the wrong place at the wrong time."

"You know I can't discuss that with you." She stood. "But I know the journalist in you can't keep from trying to get information."

I got up and pushed in my chair. "I'll let you know if I uncover anything else."

That afternoon, Misty and the girls she nannied, Tricia and Robin

Garland, arrived at Chuckie's Chicken for a late lunch, and I seated them in my section.

"When you get a chance to take a break, I have some news about Jennifer's case." Misty's eyes glittered with mischief.

"I'm intrigued," I said.

"You should be."

After I filled their drinks and submitted their order to the cook, I hustled back to their table. The girls were drawing pictures on the backs of their placemats.

"Let's talk now," I said.

Misty got up, and we huddled near the restrooms where she could still see the girls.

"I did a little spying on Tim—again." She smirked. "I was at their house picking up some new towels my mom forgot to take to her inn, and he didn't even hear the door open because he was so into his conversation with Detective Harrell."

"And?"

"Jennifer had maxed out two credit cards."

"Did he say anything about what the charges were for?"

"If he did, I didn't catch that part."

"The debt might explain how she paid for the artificial insemination, but I wonder how she planned to pay off the cards."

"What?" She blinked a few times. "I'm gonna need a little more explanation than that."

I quietly told her about my conversation with Morty at the funeral, that the mustached man was her uncle John, and how I'd purchased her photos at the drugstore.

"Wow. You've been busy." She glanced over at the table where the girls were coloring.

"So have you," I said. "Anything else I should know?"

"No," she said. "But I'd like to go to aerobics tonight. You never know what you might see—or overhear—since Leslie's teaching. Wanna come with?"

"I'm definitely in."

———

With Grandma's admonition about my workout clothes ringing in my ears, I left work and drove to Meis in Richardville to buy an aerobics outfit. After wandering around the department store, I found a mint green leotard with peach accents and coordinating tights. Since Grandma was taking care of Mom and Dad's bills, I wasn't as worried about money as I had been, so I even sprang for some scrunchy socks—without rhinestones.

When I arrived at the community center, there weren't many cars in the parking lot, even though it was nearly seven o'clock. Arrow the dog was yapping at the fence, but his creepy owner Vernon Wise wasn't lurking on the porch. This time, I didn't wait around for Misty and marched inside to face Amanda who was stationed at the door with a cash box.

"Good evening." I handed Amanda my money. "How's Leslie?"

"Why don't you ask her? You didn't seem to have a problem inserting yourself into her business before."

"And what business would that be?" I asked.

"She doesn't need you to clear her name."

"Hemi asked me to help."

Amanda pressed her lips into a thin line, and if I were a nice woman, I would've been sorry that I'd said anything. But I wasn't the least bit remorseful.

"They don't need your help."

"Jennifer deserves justice, so any investigating I do from this point on is for her." Before Amanda could say another word, I sailed into the gym where Leslie rushed up to me.

"Thanks for coming." She looked around. "As you can see, a lot of women have decided to stay away."

There were only five other ladies spread around the room. "Because it's a weeknight instead of Saturday morning?"

"I overheard someone saying a lot of regulars are missing."

"Vacations?"

She gave me a weak smile. "Have you found anything that will help prove my innocence?"

Hemi obviously hadn't told Leslie that he'd asked me to back off, which wasn't surprising since there wasn't a graceful way to explain our argument. "You're innocent until proven guilty, and I don't think the detectives have enough proof that you did anything. That rhinestone could've stuck to Jennifer's shoe and fallen off when she went downstairs."

"From a legal standpoint, you're right," Leslie said. "But if we can't find who killed Jennifer, this will ruin my reputation forever. Do you think people in this town will ever believe I'm anything but a killer who never got caught?"

"The people in this room must not think so."

"They'll never trust me to teach their children," she said. "I was home with Amanda when Tina fell, but that hasn't stopped people from believing that I pushed her—just because *she* was the witness who said I wasn't in the gym."

Misty bounced over to us. "I'm ready for my work out." She clapped with a little too much enthusiasm.

"Great." Leslie glanced at her watch. "Let's get this over with."

"*I* heard Tina Ferguson will never be normal again because of brain damage," a woman in a blue leotard whispered to her friend with a pink headband during a short break.

"I don't know how the doctors can know that until she wakes up," Headband said.

We were halfway through aerobics class, and Misty and I had an unspoken agreement that we wouldn't talk to each other so we could spy. I sipped water from my thermos and tried to appear casual.

"Do you think she'll remember who shoved her?" Blue Leotard asked.

"Maybe she tripped. Poor thing isn't very coordinated."

"What I can't figure out is why she was in the building by herself after that sweatshirt decorating class was over."

Headband stepped closer. "*I* heard she had a little something on the side with Scott Blanchard."

Could Scott and Tina have rekindled their romance in spite of what he'd told the detectives? Is that why he'd acted so guilty? But Tina had seemed genuinely happy with her husband. Unless she'd been putting on an act intended to fool me.

Blue Leotard dabbed her brow with a towel. "If that's the case, he gets around, because *I* heard from my son-in-law that Scott was seeing Jennifer Coulter, though there's no way he could've killed her because he was at the parade committee meeting."

Could Tina and Jennifer have been fighting over Scott, and the scuffle led to Jennifer's electrocution? If that were true, I couldn't understand why an average looking guy with a mullet was such a hot commodity. I could see the headline: "Spat Over Mullet Man Leads to Woman's Electrocution."

Misty turned her back to the women and looked at me with wide eyes. "Are you thinking what I'm thinking?" she mouthed.

I hoped so, but with Misty, I could never be sure. However, when I nodded, she clasped my arm, dragged me toward the library, and motioned for me to enter the dark room. I glanced over my shoulder and hoped no one was skulking in the room's nooks and crannies.

"Here's my theory," she whispered. "Tina found out Scott kissed Jennifer and was jealous. When Tina saw Jennifer at the class on Saturday morning, she followed her to the locker room to confront her. Is that where your mind was?"

"Big time. They argued, Tina shoved her, and after Jennifer fell into the water and was electrocuted, possibly accidentally, Tina covered her tracks. She framed Leslie by planting the rhinestone and lied about not seeing her prior to class."

"That makes sense." She bit her lip. "But why would someone shove Tina?"

"She could've stayed after the class last night to talk to Scott, and they got into an argument about what happened with Jennifer."

"And he pushed her because he was mad about what Tina had done to Jennifer."

"Or he's telling the truth about being home with his wife, and Tina had an accident because she's clumsy. We have great theories but no proof." I glanced down the hall. "We could sneak into Scott's office later. I don't know what we'd be looking for, but you never know what we might find."

"I'm in," she said. "When class is over, we'll pretend to go to the restroom, hide out, and wait until everyone leaves. You can pick the lock on his office door."

I laughed. "The paper clips I used to open Jennifer's apartment door are still in my purse."

"I knew I could count on you," she said. "And while we're here, you can show me the maintenance tunnel."

"Hold on." I held up a hand. "I didn't bring my gun, and I'm not thrilled about traipsing through there unarmed or without male protection. So unless you're packing heat, I'm going to say no."

She huffed. "Fine. I don't even have a gun. Tim told me I wasn't responsible enough."

"You need to stop listening to his opinions about your capabilities, because the woman who manhandled that poor lifeguard could use a firearm."

"I did scare him, didn't I?"

"You terrified me."

In the gym, music switched on, and we bopped back down the

hall to "Push It" because it was impossible to walk normally while that song was playing.

"Who needs aerobics?" I muttered. "We should just have a dance party."

An hour later, I peeked out of the restroom door. "The coast is clear," I whispered.

Misty and I tiptoed through the hallway, so our shoes didn't squeak on the chipped tile. When we reached the end, I stopped and peered around the corner at Scott's darkened office before continuing.

I tried the knob, and the door swung open. I didn't even need my paper clips. "That was easy."

"He must not keep anything valuable in here." Misty darted around the counter and into the old principal's office where she went straight to Scott's beat-up metal desk and opened the bottom drawer. It screeched, and I winced at the sound.

"I don't know what we're hoping to find," I muttered.

On top of his desk was a date book with the schedule for the community center room rentals and contact information for the renters. He had a wedding picture, but it was the other framed photo that caught my attention.

I held it so Misty could see the photo of Scott—and his looka-like brother. "Scott's an identical twin."

She studied the photo before setting it down. "It's impossible to tell them apart."

"It is, isn't it?" I leaned against the desk.

"Wait a sec." She gasped. "What if Scott's brother pretended to be him at the committee meeting on Saturday morning, so Scott could be here to confront Jennifer?"

"Or he was planning to help her with whatever she was doing because they were having an affair. Sunday, when I came here to snoop, he was on the phone with his wife talking to her about his in-laws coming for a visit and how he understood it was her family's turn because his brother had just visited," I said. "The poor guy sounded like a hostage trying to appease a captor, so I don't know how well he gets along with his wife."

Misty laughed.

"*And* Ray Winston told me Scott didn't contribute at the meeting. What if it was because he didn't know what to say *because he wasn't Scott?*"

"That makes sense," Misty said. "Scott could've flooded the basement on purpose and made the pipe look like it burst accidentally."

I considered her theory, which honestly seemed elaborately farfetched. "He'd have to know ahead of time Jennifer was coming to snoop. Although, if they were in a relationship, she might've confided in him."

"Let's say she did." Misty opened a filing cabinet and thumbed through folders. "Scott caused the flood, waited on her to arrive, and shoved her into the water to get rid of the woman carrying his child. Everyone would believe the poor girl had an accident."

"Maybe he even took her duffel bag because if it didn't have workout clothes, people might ask questions."

"Where does Tina fit into this theory?" Misty asked.

"Given Tina's history with Scott, she might've lied to protect him if she saw him here that morning. She could've even lied about seeing Jennifer," I said. "And saw an opportunity to frame Leslie. Except, that would mean Tina putting herself at risk with no apparent benefit."

"Unless Scott paid Tina to keep her mouth shut."

"She did tell me she and her husband had no savings because they spent it all on fertility treatments, so that could be motivation for accepting a bribe. She might've even demanded more money, so he shoved her down the stairs to silence her."

"Misty closed the filing cabinet drawer with a thud and

snatched the phone from Scott's desk. "I'm calling Tim. He may think we're crazy, but he can't call me any worse than stupid, and he's already implied that plenty of times in my life."

"Are you sure you want—?" A movement caught my attention, and whipping around, I gasped as Scott Blanchard hulked in the doorway. My heart squeezed to a stop.

"Hang up. Now."

CHAPTER 21

MISTY FROZE with the receiver by her ear and her finger hooked in the rotary phone's dial. I half expected to see a gun pointed at us, but Scott's hands were empty, and his facial expression appeared more annoyed than menacing. When he flicked on the lights, my heart resumed business.

"I've been listening to your harebrained theories, and before you call the cops, I'd like to defend myself." He crossed his arms. "I didn't flood the basement on purpose, and I *certainly* didn't kill Jennifer Coulter."

"Why should we believe you?" I asked as Misty replaced the receiver and took her finger off the dial.

"For starters, your twin theory is crap," he said. "My twin Steven died last year in a car accident."

"I'm sorry for your loss," Misty and I said in unison.

He nodded. "My brother Mark, who was visiting last week, is ten years younger and looks nothing like me." He reached for his wallet, flipped it open, and produced an old family picture. He pointed at a kid who didn't look at all like him. "As you can see, Mark takes after my mom, and I resemble my dad."

As Misty looked over my shoulder, I studied the older man and woman in the photo, and Scott was correct. Mark had brown hair and eyes like their mother. "Look, I'm sorry we snuck into your office," I said. "We just want to find the truth about what happened to Jennifer, and the door was unlocked . . ."

"I'll be fixing the lock sooner rather than later," he said.

"What *was* your relationship with Jennifer?" Misty asked. "We have an eyewitness who said you kissed her."

He muttered a cuss word. "Jennifer kissed *me* while she was picking my pocket for the building key."

I laughed. "You've got to be kidding."

"I wish. I thought I'd misplaced my key until I remembered that I had it right before she mauled me." His lips curled in disgust. "Now that I know people saw us, I guess I'd better tell my wife. I'd been keeping that one under my hat because, well, never mind."

"Why'd Jennifer want the key?" I asked.

"She said she wanted to look for clues to what happened to Phineas. I have no idea what she thought she'd find after all these years, but I told her I'd have let her search during business hours if she'd have asked. She gave the key back after that."

"Was Jennifer planning to explore the community center on Saturday morning?" I asked.

"Probably, but I'm not certain," he said. "After she kissed me, I avoided her like the plague."

"What about Tina Ferguson?" Misty asked. "Is there any truth to the rumor that you've been seeing her again?"

He snorted. "Absolutely not. Tina's happily married. We're ancient history, and after what she went through with her first husband, I don't think she'd do anything to jeopardize her marriage now that she's finally content." He pointed to his door. "Are we done here? I'd like to go home to my wife."

Misty and I filed out of his office.

"One more question," I said. "Did Jennifer say anything at all about what she was hoping to find?"

"She mentioned a sealed staircase and tunnels," he said. "I

thought she was crazy, but as I told you before, this building belongs to the community, and as long as she wasn't going to do any damage, I told her she could snoop all she wanted."

I studied him. "Are you not aware that there's a maintenance tunnel running under this building—and that an entire stairwell was sealed off after a fire?"

"You're kidding, right?"

"Nope. Duke Talbert and I found them when we were ghost hunting."

"Man, he didn't mention that when he returned the key. He probably figured I already knew." Scott shook his head. "I've got to find a new job. This building is creeping me out." He held the outside door open for us as if he wanted to make sure we exited.

"I'm curious about something else," I said. "How many people have keys to this building?"

Scott locked the door and pocketed the key. "Your guess is as good as mine. I heard they didn't change the locks when they renovated, so who knows how many are floating around. I guess that's why I wasn't all that concerned about the broken lock on my office door. I figured half the town could get in, and like you said, I don't keep anything valuable there." He waved and walked down the street. "You two stay out of trouble, and keep me off your suspect list."

"We'll try," Misty said as we walked toward our cars. "That was nice of him not to get mad at us."

"Maybe it was too nice."

"What do you mean?"

"He either truly has nothing to hide, or he was playing it cool and trying to steer us in the wrong direction," I said. "But my gut says he's telling the truth."

"Mine too." Misty unlocked her car.

"Tomorrow, I'll verify with the state health department that they have a death certificate for his brother Steve."

"Okay, but if Scott were guilty and wanted to cover his tracks, he could've killed us to make it look like Phineas had claimed two more victims." She opened her Firebird's door. "What'd you have in mind when you were asking about the keys?"

"Something's not sitting right with me about Flossie Perkins since she's the one spreading the rumors about ghosts."

"Flossie Perkins." Misty snorted and got into her car. "She's the sweetest woman you'll ever meet. You wouldn't even be *considering* her as a suspect if she'd been *your* second-grade teacher."

"She probably still has a key to the building."

"*That's* why you asked Scott about the keys? Even if Flossie has one, that doesn't mean she used it to sneak in and murder Jennifer. It's more likely Leslie or Tina killed Jennifer." She started the car. "I'll see you later."

As Misty drove away, I sighed. I hadn't meant to offend her with my suggestion that her beloved teacher might be guilty, but I had to consider everything.

Misty would have to get over it.

I glanced at the dashboard clock, and since it was only a little after nine, I drove to Grandma's. Though she was an early riser, she didn't bother to go to bed until around midnight because she claimed she'd get bed sores if she slept more than six hours.

When I parked in front of her house, she was rocking on her porch swing, while lightning bugs flitted around the yard.

"What are you doing here at this time of night?" She sipped from her teacup.

"Were you planning on going to bed early?" I sat next to her.

"I see you took my advice and got one of those cute aerobics outfits. It's a big improvement over your ugly sweatpants," she said. "It's nice to know that someone in my family listens—at least once in a while."

"Thanks."

"Don't thank me. Buy more so you can find a husband."

"I should pick my spouse based on his approval of how *I* look in a leotard? I hope I have more attractive qualities than that."

"You do. At least, most of the time. But men are visual, and they'll like what they see if you take my advice."

"Could we—?"

"Talk about something else? How about Duke?"

"What about him?"

"He's too good looking for you."

"Just when I was feeling better about myself," I muttered. "Grandma steamrolls my self-confidence."

"You're an attractive girl, but he's movie-star handsome. I bet he beats ladies off with a stick. You want women throwing themselves at your husband all the time?"

"Marry someone ugly. Got it."

"Oh, for heaven's sake. That's not what I meant. You have to look at him every day for the rest of your life. Just don't marry a man who's so good looking you feel like you can't measure up."

"How do you know that's how I feel?" I focused on my fingernails' chipped paint and hoped Grandma wouldn't comment on that too.

"You're not arguing."

"Duke and I are friends and fellow journalists. No one is talking about marriage."

"It's too bad the asparagus spear is engaged," she said.

"He has a name." I gritted my teeth.

"*Hemi* would be a good match for you. Cute, but not so good looking that you'd need to look over your shoulder all the time." Grandma chuckled. "You like him, and it's taking every last bit of your self-control to keep from smacking me when I call him the asparagus spear."

"He's an acquaintance, and I'm not looking for a husband."

"He's not available, and you wouldn't take my advice if he were." She set her teacup on the windowsill. "What brings you by?"

I told her what Misty and I had learned from Scott and why I was considering Flossie Perkins might be involved.

Grandma rocked in silence.

"Well?" I asked.

"I'm thinking." She swung back and forth while I studied the lightning bugs and wondered if I should've kept Grandma out of this situation. "Do you think a seventy-two-year-old woman could overpower a girl in her twenties and shove her into the water?"

"Flossie's tall—and in good shape," I said. "I watched her at aerobics."

Grandma rocked some more. "Years ago, there was a rumor Flossie never got over Phineas's death because they were such good friends. Judy Beeson was the school cafeteria director at that time. Seems like I remember her saying she witnessed some strange things involving Flossie, but it's been so long, I can't remember. In fact, she may not've told me details at all—since she tries not to gossip."

"Do you think Judy would talk to me about Flossie?"

"Possibly, but we'll have to convince her we're not idly gossiping."

"We?"

"You'd cut your old grandma out of a critical conversation with her best friend? After I gave you the lead?"

"I'm sorry." I stood. "Let's talk to Judy as soon as possible."

"I'll call her first thing tomorrow morning and let you know what she says." She got off the swing. "But get plenty of sleep tonight. You look tired."

"Yes, Grandma."

When Grandma said first thing in the morning, she wasn't kidding. I awoke to the phone clanging at five after seven, and I was ordered to report to Judy Beeson's at promptly eight o'clock, where I would be expected to assist Grandma and Judy in preparing casseroles for Tina Ferguson's family since Tina was Judy's great-niece by marriage.

Grandma also gave me strict instructions to allow her to question Judy about Flossie Perkins.

Judy lived on the outskirts of Wildcat Springs in a brick ranch, and when I arrived at 7:59, Grandma's Eldorado was parked in Judy's driveway.

I didn't even have a chance to knock before Judy swung the door open. "Good morning, Bobbi Sue. You're right on time." She thrust a coffee mug at me. "Isadora told me you're not a morning person and that you take your coffee black."

I blinked and took the *I Love Lucy* mug. "Thank you."

"Come in, come in." Judy led me to the kitchen, where Grandma was at the stove browning hamburger. A row of disposable pans waited like soldiers on Judy's dining room table. The kitchen counter displayed cans of cream soups, a pile of vegetables, and a stack of assorted pasta boxes. Judy pointed to an onion waiting on a cutting board. "Wash your hands, and then chop that onion, please."

"Okay." I set the mug on the counter and went to the sink. "How's Tina doing?"

"We had a wonderful answer to prayer last night." Judy unhooked a pot hanging on the rack above her island. "She's out of her coma and asking for her husband and son."

"Praise the Lord," Grandma said.

"Does she remember what happened?" I dried my hands and peeled the onion skin.

"I'm afraid not, but apparently, that's not unusual. She does remember everything else about her life, like her husband and son, though the last thing she recalls is going into the community center for her sweatshirt decorating class. The doctor told her she may never recollect the accident."

"The police are certain it was an accident?" I asked.

Grandma raised her eyebrows but, to my surprise, didn't comment.

"Oh my, yes." Judy filled the pot with water. "The class instructor thought she was the last one to leave, but Tina must've gone to the restroom before she tripped and fell on her way out. She's been open about having bowel troubles, so she might've been in the restroom for a while. If she had an attack, the poor instructor probably had no idea Tina was in there, shut off the lights, and locked the building."

I tossed the onion skins in the garbage and wondered if the police were making the right call for Tina. What if it wasn't an accident, and her killer came back to finish the job?

Grandma drained the hamburger and set the skillet on a trivet. "With everything that's happened lately, I think the community should've closed the building."

Judy set the pot on the stove and turned on the burner. "I wholeheartedly agree. Ever since folks started believing the school was haunted, things have gotten even worse." She pointed at the refrigerator. "There are chicken breasts in there that I thawed last night. Cook those, please, Isadora."

Grandma retrieved the chicken. "Speaking of the haunting, Flossie Perkins is convinced that Phineas Jones is a ghost. Jennifer Coulter wasn't even cold, and Flossie was telling Bobbi Sue that Phineas had done it."

Judy lifted the lid before replacing it. "The watched pot never boils." She faced me. "Never you mind about Flossie. She's a lovely woman, but Phineas's death hit her hard because they were friends, and she's not been quite right in the head since she and that other teacher found him."

"That would be a shock—walking into your classroom and finding a dead man." I pushed the sliced onion aside.

"Cut the red pepper next, dear," Judy said. "And you're right. I haven't thought about this for a long time, but I used to work in that old school as the cafeteria director. One Friday night, I realized my wallet had fallen out of my purse, and I needed it the next morning, so I went to my office to pick it up. As I was leaving, I spotted Flossie in the hallway, but she didn't see me. As I was about to say hello, I heard her say, 'Phineas, I wish I'd known how you were feeling. Why didn't you tell me you were suffering? Nadia wouldn't have wanted you to do this either.'"

Grandma glanced at me. "Who was Nadia?"

"His long-lost love." Judy checked the pot again, and this time, she dumped a box of bow-tie pasta into the water. "Now, I didn't think much of that. It's not all that unusual for a grieving person to talk to someone they've lost, and even though it'd been ten years since Phineas had died, Flossie still missed her friend."

"I talk to Norman all the time, even though I know he's with the good Lord and can't hear me," Grandma said.

"Exactly," Judy said. "I do the same with my mom. I reckoned Flossie wouldn't want me interrupting, and I certainly didn't want to embarrass her, so I waited until she passed and quietly left."

"Did you hear anything else?" Grandma tossed a chicken breast into the skillet.

Judy stirred the pasta. "Flossie said that she was having trouble finding a good man, and Vernon Wise had been hitting on her, but she wasn't interested." Judy stirred the pasta. "I even remember her saying Vernon was wearing the cologne Phineas used to wear because all the ladies liked it, but it had no effect on her."

"Can you blame her?" I sliced the red pepper. "Was Vernon as creepy then as he is now?"

"Yes," Grandma said but shot me a warning look that I interpreted to mean that my comment could be considered too gossipy for Judy's taste.

I bit my tongue, kept slicing, and wondered why Flossie had blamed Phineas's ghost for the cologne smell when it'd probably just been Vernon hanging around trying to impress her.

"I agree about Vernon, though it seems uncharitable to say so,"

Judy said. "But Flossie went on to ask Phineas to scare Vernon while he was cleaning in the building at night. She was hoping he'd leave her alone."

"I didn't know Vernon worked at the school." Grandma flipped a chicken breast.

"He took Phineas's custodial job after he died," Judy said.

"It's funny how she was walking around the building by herself if she was trying to avoid Vernon," I said.

"I thought the same thing, but when I left that night, Vernon's car wasn't there," Judy said. "He must've finished early or taken the night off, so Flossie felt safe."

"Did you hear anything else?" Grandma asked.

"No. Flossie disappeared after that, and I got out of there. But I heard more than one person say they'd come into the building on a weekend and caught her wandering around the halls talking to herself."

"Do you think she still does?" Grandma asked.

Judy shook her head. "It wouldn't surprise me, though the problem got better after she married Ted Perkins. He gave her something else to focus on, and she helped raise his poor, motherless children." Judy pointed to a green pepper. "Chop that next, Bobbi Sue."

While I cut the green pepper, I considered Flossie as a suspect. With her fondness for Phineas, it seemed unlikely that she'd kill Jennifer, who was trying to clear Phineas's good name. Wouldn't Flossie support that?

Unless Jennifer had uncovered information that threatened to ruin her friend Phineas's reputation, and Flossie had silenced her forever.

CHAPTER 22

"Nita," I said to my cat, "why am I letting Grandma get into my head about Duke?"

Nita stared at me from the hallway while I curled my hair in the bathroom in preparation for my date, but she had no answer as to why my enthusiasm about going out with Duke had evaporated like every bit of moisture in the unusually dry air.

I set the curling iron on the counter, fluffed my hair, and sprayed it. "I don't know why Misty thinks I can't style my own hair," I muttered. "It looks fine."

I grabbed my purse and headed downstairs to wait for Duke to pick me up, but as I was walking out the door, the phone rang. For a second, I considered letting the machine get it, but ever since Mom and Dad had disappeared, each time the phone rang, I hoped it was them.

I raced into the kitchen and answered.

"Hey. It's Duke."

"Are you running late?" I glanced at my watch.

"I'm sorry, but I have to cancel."

Cancel—not reschedule. I wrapped the cord around my wrist. "You couldn't have told me this a couple of hours ago?"

"I called earlier, but you didn't answer."

"You could've left a message."

"I was afraid you wouldn't see it," he said. "I had something come up for work, and I need to take care of it right away."

If there were a contest for being as vague as possible, Duke had just won. "I see. Is this your new project about haunted buildings?"

"No, it's something confidential I'm working on." He cleared his throat. "I'll, uh, call you . . . sometime."

I freed my wrist from the phone cord. "We both know you won't, so let's agree to say it's been nice knowing you."

There was a beat of silence. "Take care, Bobbi Sue."

"You too."

I hung up the phone. "I can't believe I bought a new dress for that idiot." I stomped back upstairs where I changed into acid wash jeans and a striped T-shirt that'd seen better days. There was no way I was going to wear that cute little dress to Tate's Place, because while I could use some company, I certainly wasn't in the mood for male attention.

"I'm bummed Duke cancelled on you at the last minute. He seemed so interested," Misty said from her usual stool at Tate's Place.

"Grandma scared him away." I told her about our dinner.

Misty stared at me. "You most *definitely* did this on purpose."

"What?"

"You let Duke have dinner at her house because you *wanted* your grandma to scare him away."

"Get real. Why would I do that?"

Misty's eyes glimmered as she looked at Kurt. "Why do *you* think she did it?"

"I can think of one good reason." He winked at Misty.

"Neither of you have proof that I did anything," I said. "And people say *I* have an overactive imagination."

"I'm *so* sure she let a gorgeous specimen of a man eat dinner at her grandma's house after a few dates and had no idea that woman's brutal honesty might be a deal breaker for any sane man." Misty rolled her eyes. "You don't introduce a guy you're serious about to a grandma like yours unless he's already hopelessly in love with you."

"My grandma's a nice lady." I had no idea why I said that. Even *I* didn't believe me.

"Nice?" Kurt leaned against the bar and gazed at Misty. "Is this the woman who scared you so badly you made yourself sick on Oreos?"

"Uh-huh."

Kurt directed his icy blue gaze at me. "You sabotaged yourself."

"She's my grandmother. I have to respect her wishes, and she wished to meet Duke."

He guffawed. "It doesn't make any difference to me if you date Duke or not. Just be honest with Misty—and yourself."

"She did it because of Hemi Miller," she whispered.

"What?" I sputtered. "That's absurd. *He's engaged.*"

"I don't know. I witnessed the argument you and Hemi had in here a few days ago." Kurt turned to Misty. "They were going at it, and he reached down and tipped up her chin."

"Like he wanted to kiss her?" Misty leaned forward.

Kurt nodded slowly and smirked. "But couldn't. Then, they both stomped off."

"Why do you never tell me these things?" Misty whined.

"Because they're not worth discussing," I snapped.

"She's hopeless—and in total denial," Misty said. "You should've heard how mad she got at her grandma for comparing Hemi to an asparagus spear."

Kurt guffawed—again.

"That, I won't deny. It's rude to compare people's bodies to

167

vegetables and fruit." I drained my Coke and slid it across the counter. "Refill, please, Kurt. And not another word about Hemi—from either of you."

Kurt took my glass.

"How's the case coming?" Misty asked.

I told her what I'd learned about Tina's recovery and what Judy had told me about Flossie. I'd even confirmed that Scott Blanchard's brother had passed away. "I keep hitting dead ends."

"I hope you're not still considering Mrs. Perkins a suspect," Misty said.

"Unless Jennifer stumbled into something that portrayed Phineas in a bad light, and Flossie didn't want it to come out, I don't see her having a motive." I hoped that answer satisfied Misty because I wasn't convinced Flossie was innocent.

"What's next?" she asked.

I weighed my options. "I'm going to aerobics class tomorrow morning."

"Good idea. You never know what you might overhear. I'd join you, but tomorrow is the parade, and remember, I'm the grand marshal." She practiced her Soybean Queen wave.

Like I could forget.

But I simply said, "Excuse me. I need to go to the ladies' room." In one motion, I swiveled, hopped off my stool, and plowed right into a man's chest. "I'm sor—"

Hemi.

Misty produced a fake cough that did nothing to disguise her giggle.

"Hello, Roberta." He stepped out of my way.

"*Roberta?* Are you trying to act like your mother, or are you just a pompous jerk?" I gritted my teeth. Why hadn't I left my new dress on? The outfit I was wearing wasn't exactly confrontation worthy.

"Could be both." He shrugged. "Hey, Misty. Kurt."

"Hi," she said. "How's Leslie?"

"She's fine. Her sister Lorraine is visiting, and since they're having girl time, I'm a bachelor tonight." He sat next to Misty—on the stool I'd vacated. Then, he looked at me. "Please don't let me stop you from wherever you were going in such a hurry."

I lifted my chin, sailed toward the restroom, and was about to close myself into a stall when Misty barged in.

"You could've warned me Hemi was right behind me." I gripped the stall door.

Her eyes glimmered. "You told us not to say another word about him."

"That would've been the exception."

She leaned closer to the mirror and fluffed her hair. "If it makes you feel any better, he tried to pretend he doesn't care, but he watched you walk all the way to the bathroom."

Maybe my outfit wasn't so bad after all.

"It doesn't, because he's engaged to Leslie." I slammed the stall door so hard it bounced open.

"Which bothers you."

I yanked the door shut. "It doesn't matter what I think." I sagged against the door, glad that Misty couldn't see me blinking away tears. "It's reality." I hoped my voice sounded as nonchalant as I wanted it to.

"I know, and I'm sorry."

"Don't be." I swiped moisture from my cheek. "Because I'm not."

That night, when I arrived at home, I was passing my dad's office when I noticed the fax machine whirring. My heart thumped, and I flipped on the lights and raced over to the machine. Were Mom and Dad finally contacting Rochelle and me?

I seized the paper, and when I read the cover sheet, my shoulders slumped. It was from Duke. My dad had given him the fax number, his note explained, when they'd met while Duke was researching *Close Encounters in the USA*. He thought I might like to see the article he'd found from a 1935 Indianapolis newspaper.

Had I dismissed Duke too quickly? Should I have been more understanding when he'd called? No. This gesture was a sign that he cared about finding the truth. He didn't want to date me. Shaking off the twinge of regret, I focused on the article.

Circus Performer Found Guilty of Gas City Robbery

Gas City, Ind., Jan. 18—A jury found William Allen, 24, guilty of stealing nearly $15,000 in jewelry from the home of Mr. and Mrs. Jack Smythe on May 6 of last year while the Wheeling Brothers Circus was in Gas City. Allen was a performer with the traveling circus. In September, police recovered the Smythe family jewelry in Allen's Indianapolis boarding house and arrested him shortly after.

Allen is also suspected in a Hidden Shores theft of nearly $20,000 in jewelry. This robbery took place on May 13, 1934, the final day the circus was in Hidden Shores, Indiana. However, Allen has not been formally charged with this crime, and the jewelry has not been found. Authorities suspect his sister, equestrian performer Nadia Allen, may be his accomplice, but she disappeared prior to her brother's arrest and has not been seen since.

My mind raced while I considered the article's information. Had Nadia taken the jewelry from Hidden Shores with the hope of using the money to free herself from her brother's influence? Then, I remembered her words.

The secret with which I have entrusted you.

Had Nadia given Phineas the jewelry for safekeeping? Had Jennifer come to the same conclusion and suspected that Phineas had stashed the jewelry in the tunnel or the sealed stairwell? Had she been looking for the jewelry?

But more importantly, had Jennifer's search led to her murder?

The next morning at aerobics class, the community center gym was crowded because Shira had returned from her face-lift leave. I'd just found a spot toward the back where I could keep an eye on everyone when Leslie sidled up to me.

"If Shira hadn't recovered earlier than expected, they would've fired me from this job, too," Leslie muttered.

"Any word on your teaching position?"

"The school board is meeting later this week."

"I'm so sorry."

"It's not your fault," she said. "You've tried to help."

"Your sister didn't want to join you this morning?"

"How'd you know about her?" Leslie eyed me with a hint of suspicion.

"I ran into Hemi last night at Tate's Place." *Literally.*

"Oh." She looked around. "Lorraine hates exercise and wanted to sleep in."

Next to us, Flossie Perkins was stretching. When she stopped, she put her hand on her back. "I don't know if these old bones can handle this today."

"All right, everyone!" Shira yelled. "I'm thrilled to be here. Let's give Leslie Enright a hand for taking over while I was recovering." Shira clapped with enthusiasm that felt fake, but the rest of the women didn't even try.

"Whooo-hooo!" I yelled.

"I'm ready to march through a warmup, are you?" Shira asked.

"Yes!" several women shouted in unison.

Shira bent over her boombox, and "Beat It" blasted out. "Annnddd . . . march forward, forward, forward. Clap. And backward, back, back. Clap. And forward, forward, forward."

I clapped, marched, and glanced at Flossie who was keeping up despite her achy body. When class was over, I'd ask her more about Phineas and Nadia and watch her reaction to see if she had any idea about the jewelry.

I trooped forward. People had blamed Flossie's poor teacher friend Nella Aidan when Phineas most likely had killed himself. He'd probably felt guilty about holding on to stolen property for a woman who'd used him.

Wait a second. Nella Aidan.

And backward, back, back.

I almost tripped over my own feet as the letters in the name *Nella Aidan* ping-ponged through my brain, and I realized why Nadia Allen's full name had seemed familiar the first time I'd seen it.

Nadia Allen spelled backward was Nella Aidan.

CHAPTER 23

WHILE I CONTINUED MARCHING through the aerobics routine to "Beat It," I toyed with my theory that Nadia and Nella were the same woman.

Flossie told me Phineas met Nadia when the circus came to town, and he'd pined for her after she never returned. But what if she'd come back, and no one realized it? If Nadia gave Phineas the jewelry to hide for her and didn't want to share the money from selling it, she could've reversed her name to Nella Aidan, pretended to be a teacher, and taken a job at the school where Phineas was working in hopes of finding the jewelry on her own.

Flossie had described Nella as dumpy—with thick glasses. Could Nadia have put on weight and glasses to disguise herself so Phineas wouldn't recognize her? Had she befriended him in hopes of finding the treasure without having to rekindle a romance? What if she'd killed Phineas because he'd refused to tell her where he'd hidden the jewels? Had Nadia/Nella eventually found the jewelry? Or was it still tucked away?

"Beat It" ended.

"Mrs. Perkins," I whispered. "Your teacher friend who found Phineas . . . the day he died. Is she still alive?"

Confusion flitted through Flossie's expression. "No idea. We

173

didn't keep in touch." She dabbed sweat from her forehead. "A year or so after Nella left, I called the school where she claimed she had a job to check on her, but they'd never heard of her. Why?"

"Just thinking," I murmured as "Danger Zone" blasted from Shira's boom box.

I glanced at Flossie again. What if all the times she'd been seen wandering through the school were because she'd been searching for Phineas's hidden treasure? Had she made up the ghostly rumors to keep people away from the school? Had she killed Phineas and murdered Jennifer to keep the truth from coming out?

Even if this were true, how could I prove a beloved elementary school teacher might be hiding a deadly secret?

Flossie was still on my mind when Shira finally gave us a break. Wondering if Jennifer had ever mentioned her suspicions about Phineas to Shira, I took a drink and moseyed over to chat with her. "How's your friend Tina?"

"Oh, thank you so much for asking," Shira drawled. "She has a broken leg, and because of her head injury, the poor thing can't remember anything that happened, or why she was in the building alone."

"I heard she went to the restroom, and the instructor didn't realize anyone was still in the building."

"Yes, that's what we *think* happened, but Tina only remembers coming in for the class. After that, the next thing she recalls is waking up in the hospital." Shira bent over, opened her tote bag, and withdrew a towel. "Thankfully, the doctors think she'll make a full recovery." She dabbed her face.

"Thank goodness. I was wondering—" I clamped my mouth

shut. In the bottom of Shira's bag was a camera with a blue and white woven strap and a pin—exactly like Grandma's.

I ripped my gaze away from Shira's bag while my mind spun.

"Wondering?" Shira asked.

"If Tina needs anything," I blurted and took a sip of water. "Just feeling a little dizzy and lost my train of thought."

"Stay hydrated. This building is stuffy." Her eyes darkened. "To answer your question, Tina's family and friends have taken care of everything she needs."

"Good to know." I walked back toward Leslie in a daze and considered the possibilities. Jennifer could've met Shira and given her the camera last Saturday morning. Shira could've found Jennifer's abandoned bag and decided to keep a perfectly good camera for herself. Or the worst-case scenario was that Shira fought with Jennifer and their struggle ended with Jennifer's electrocution.

"Leslie, may I talk to you in the hall?" I whispered as I picked up my purse.

"Sure." She followed me out of the gym, and we stopped next to the old principal's office. "What's wrong?"

"Shira has the camera that Jennifer Coulter bought from my grandma in her bag. I'd know the strap and pin anywhere."

Leslie blinked a few times. "And . . . you think that means she killed Jennifer?"

"Possibly," I said. "Tina spotted Jennifer with a duffel bag, but when I found her, there was no bag. Shira must've taken it because Jennifer's camera was inside."

"Why wouldn't she get rid of the camera if she killed Jennifer?"

I thought for a moment. "Because she wanted to finish the roll of film so she could develop it to see what Jennifer had photographed?" I chewed my lip. "I think Jennifer was searching for stolen jewelry that Phineas hid for the woman he loved because she needed the money to pay off her credit card debt. Shira found out and wanted the money for herself. She must've been hoping Jennifer's pictures would lead her to the jewelry Phineas hid."

"But Shira went boating with her family last Saturday morning."

"She could've killed Jennifer before they left for the day."

Leslie glanced over her shoulder at the gym entrance. "I'd love it if you were right, but I doubt Detective Melchor will be impressed. Do you have *any* other proof?"

"Not yet. I need to get my hands on that camera."

Leslie stared at the old trophy case as if she were contemplating something. "I didn't want to say this to you in front of Amanda, but when I came in here last Saturday morning, I felt like . . . someone was already here with me. After I heard the rumors about the building being haunted, I thought that's what I'd sensed. Also, when I was turning on the lights in the gym, I heard some rustling, so I told myself it was a mouse."

"Or it was Shira."

"Leslie!" One of the women from the class made a beeline for us. "Oh, good. You're still here."

"Why?"

"Shira needs you to finish the class."

"Why?"

"She's feeling light-headed and needs to go home."

Of course she does. Leslie and I glanced at each other.

"Come on." The woman put her hand on the small of Leslie's back and steered her toward the gym. "You did great filling in. Shira said so herself, and you know how much she likes to be in control, so that's a huge compliment." She tittered. "You didn't hear this from me, but rumor has it, Shira spied on the classes you taught."

"*All* of them?" Leslie glanced at me.

"Every. Single. One. Talk about being a control freak."

With wide eyes, Leslie looked over her shoulder at me.

"I'll call for help," I mouthed and pantomimed. Before Shira could exit the gym, I slipped into Scott's unlocked office and ducked behind his desk where I pulled the phone down on the floor next to me along with a phone book.

With trembling fingers, I thumbed through the pages, found the number for the Richard County Sheriff's Department, and dialed. When a receptionist answered, I asked for Detective Harrell.

"She's not available," the bored-sounding woman said.

I peeked around the desk to see if Shira had left the gym, but the hallway outside the office was empty. "Detective Melchor?"

"He's not available either."

"This is Bobbi Sue Baxter, and I need to talk to one of them as soon as possible because I may know who killed Jennifer Coulter —and why."

"Is there a number where you could be reached?" Nothing in her tone indicated excitement over my statement.

I rattled off my home number—and the community center's number printed on the phone's label. "How soon will they be available?"

"I don't know. I'll give them your message. Have a nice day." She hung up.

Clenching my teeth, I replaced the receiver and peered over the cabinet to check for Shira while I contemplated who else to call. Misty was getting ready for the parade, and Rochelle and Jason had gone to his family's cottage at Lake Hideaway for the weekend.

Someone needed to know what I was about to do.

I dialed the number for Miller's Books. While the phone rang, I kept my eyes on the hall.

"Miller's Books. Hemi speaking."

"I'm at the community center. Shira Elliot may've killed Jennifer—but I need proof." I told him about Grandma's camera, the stolen jewelry, and what I'd learned from Leslie. "I tried calling Detective Melchor, but he and his partner aren't available." I glanced out into the hallway where Shira was finally exiting the gym. "Gotta go. I'm following Shira."

"Bobbi S—"

I slammed down the receiver.

Clutching her bag to her side, Shira strode past the trophy cases toward the restrooms and locker rooms instead of heading for the exit. I scurried down the hall and spotted her entering the basement stairwell. Rushing forward, I caught the door before it closed and slipped through. She charged into Phineas's office, and when she secured the door, I squatted underneath the window and peered inside.

Shira dragged the lockers away from the wall, opened the manhole, and disappeared into the tunnel. I rooted through my purse and found my penlight in the bottom before I tiptoed into the office where I crept to the tunnel entrance and listened.

Hearing nothing, I clenched the flashlight with my teeth, grasped the ladder, and descended. When I reached the bottom, I listened until I heard a noise to my right, which was the path that led away from the school. Feeling like a lab rat in a maze, I flipped on the penlight and inched through the tunnel. A clank and a scrape caused me to freeze, and my flashlight flickered, indicating a dying battery.

I edged closer to the noise, stopped, and peered around a corner. A small camping lantern was propped against a wall, and Shira was removing bricks from the tunnel wall behind a pipe and setting them aside. Since she was having no difficulty extracting them, they must've already been loosened.

A creak caused me to whip back around the corner, and my penlight flickered one last time and died.

"Shira, what in the Sam Hill are ya doing?"

CHAPTER 24

I DIDN'T NEED light to recognize Vernon Wise's gravelly voice. I pressed against the tunnel's brick wall and listened for Shira's answer.

"Bobbi Sue Baxter knows," Shira said.

"Knows what?"

I peeked around the corner where Vernon and Shira stood facing each other. The lantern he was holding illuminated a hollow behind the pipe above their heads and a small brick pile at their feet.

"I was talking to her at aerobics class, and when I got a towel out of my bag, she saw the camera. I don't know how she knows it was Jennifer's, but she does. I feel it."

"She ain't got no proof it ain't yours," he said. "What if someone caught you? Your paranoia is gonna ruin everything I've spent my life workin' for."

"I'm not paranoid!" Shira curled her fingers into a fist. "Bobbi Sue could've seen Jennifer with the camera, or who knows? She might've told her something about the jewelry!"

"You don't know that."

"After Bobbi Sue looked into my bag, she took Leslie Enright out of class and never came back. I faked feeling sick to get Leslie to finish teaching, so I could hide the camera."

"Why were you carryin' around that camera in the first place? You've had plenty of time to get rid of it." Vernon scowled. "I thought you was smart."

"I was waiting for a chance to bring it here to hide. If people ever found it, they'd assume Jennifer stashed it. But the other night when I sneaked into the building, Tina caught me."

"And you couldn'ta lied about whatcha were doin' here?"

"I tried, but she knew something was wrong because she saw me dart behind the curtain in the gym last Saturday morning. When she asked about it, I told her I was there to spy on Leslie Enright who was teaching my class. She believed me until she saw me on Monday night. She got so upset when she was demanding answers that she tripped down the stairs."

"Lucky for you Tina don't remember anything."

"But I'm terrified she will," Shira said. "That's why we need to lay low for a while. Wait."

"I been waiting for almost forty years. I ain't waiting any longer. We take care of Tina. And Bobbi Sue. I know a thing or two about cars. How 'bout I cut their brake lines?"

"No one was supposed to die." Shira sobbed. "All I wanted was for Jennifer to give me her bag because I was afraid she'd taken the jewelry. When I tried to grab it, she lost her balance. I didn't know the water would electrocute her." She sank onto the floor.

"Pull yourself together. We're about to get rich."

Jennifer must've been on her way to retrieve the jewelry when Shira had intercepted her.

Vernon withdrew a bag from the hidden compartment and dumped the contents into his palm. Gold and diamonds sparkled. "I got a buyer coming this afternoon to take this jewelry off our hands, and we're home free, but if you can't handle yourself—"

"Then what?" Shira stood.

"You'd better watch your back."

"Don't you dare threaten me," she spat out. "You'd have never found the jewelry if I hadn't come along and helped."

"You wouldn'ta even known about them jewels if I hadn't told you about Phin's confession and Nadia's backstabbing in his suicide note."

"You owe my family for keeping that a secret all these years," she said through clenched teeth as she pressed her pointer finger into his chest. "All Mom ever wanted was closure, and you could've given it to her by showing her his note the day you found it stuck behind his desk. Instead, you let her go on thinking he might've been murdered."

A few seconds passed as they glared at each other.

Finally, Shira stood on her tiptoes and shoved the camera into the opening. "Help me put these bricks back, so we can get out of here," she snapped.

Vernon shoved the jewelry bag into his pocket and growled a few cuss words but handed her a brick.

While they were distracted with fixing the wall, I needed to get away. But they were standing between the tunnel's exterior exit and me, so I'd have to escape through the basement entrance before they blocked it with the lockers.

But with a dead flashlight, I'd have to navigate through the dark.

Pressing my hand against the tunnel wall, I let the bricks guide me in the direction I'd come. The ground was uneven, so as much as I wanted to run, I had to tread carefully so I didn't trip and make noise.

I pressed forward, and my toe caught on a brick. Before I could catch myself on the wall, I stumbled forward and lost my balance. Though I stifled the cry of pain from my knee smacking into the ground, the noise of my fall echoed through the tunnel.

"What was that?" Shira asked.

"Prolly just a rat."

"It's too big for a rat. Someone else is here."

I leaped up, and clinging to the wall, tried to move faster, though my tights had ripped, and blood was dribbling down my shin. At last, I rounded the corner, and the light from Phineas's office illuminated the ladder, so I increased my speed.

"It's Bobbi Sue!" Shira yelled.

I grabbed the ladder and lifted myself up, but before I reached the top, Vernon snared my leg.

"You ain't getting' away," he snarled and tried to jerk me off the ladder.

Tightening my grip on the rungs, I forced my legs to go limp, and in the split second he loosened his hold, I kicked backward, slamming my heel into his face.

Crack.

He swore while I shimmied up the ladder. "Catch her!"

Hoisting myself out of the opening, I ran through the basement, past the locker rooms, and toward the stairs.

"Stop, Bobbi Sue. Let's make a deal," Shira yelled. "Vernon and I can give you a cut of the jewelry money. You don't need to report us."

I pounded upstairs. "I don't make deals with killers." I didn't slow my pace, though my knee was aching.

"I didn't mean to kill Jennifer," she wailed. "And I never touched Tina. You've taken aerobics classes with her. Haven't you seen how clumsy she is?"

"Give it up, Shira," Vernon said. "We gotta get rid of her."

Praying Detectives Melchor or Harrell had gotten my message and arrived, I burst into the empty hallway and limped past the stairwell and trophy case. No music was coming from the darkened gym.

Instead, I heard the high school's marching band playing "You're a Grand Old Flag" outside because the Independence Day Parade had kicked off. I raced into the sunshine where families lined the sidewalk on Main Street. Small children wiggled in red wagons, and parents and grandparents sat in lawn chairs and waved American flags in time with the music. The scent of greasy elephant ears lingered on the breeze.

The Marching Wildcats passed in their blue and gray uniforms heading north into downtown Wildcat Springs. Behind them was a float sponsored by the upcoming senior class of 1989, and students lobbed candy at the kids squatted next to the street.

Though most people were engrossed in the parade, necks craned when I passed, and one elderly woman shouted, "Miss, do you need help? You're bleeding!"

Following the parade route, I sprinted behind the crowd and crossed Park Road. Ducking behind the oak tree next to my church, I spotted Vernon and Shira meandering behind the people lining Main Street. Shira shaded her eyes and looked back and forth while Vernon plodded a few steps behind her as if they were trying not to show they were together.

"Where's a cop when you need one?" I muttered.

A young woman with a chubby baby on her hip stopped Shira and pointed toward me. Shira waved the woman away and escaped onto Park Road with Vernon at her heels. Had they given up on chasing me and were trying to get away without calling attention to themselves?

Sucking in a deep breath, I darted past the historical society as I spotted Kurt idling along Pearl Street in his red Mustang convertible leading the parade. Dressed in her pale-yellow gown, Misty smiled and waved from the back. An idea rocketed into my mind, and before I could change my mind, I dodged a pudgy man holding lemon shake-ups, leaped over a fire hydrant, and sprinted toward Kurt's car.

Then, I hurtled over the passenger door and landed face down in the back seat.

"Oooff!" I groaned as the crowd gasped. At least I hadn't

missed and been creamed in front of half the town. I rolled over and looked up at Misty.

"What're you doing?" she shrieked as she yanked her gauzy skirt away from my bloody knee.

"That was quite a move," Kurt muttered.

"Shira killed Jennifer over stolen jewelry that Phineas Jones hid in the tunnel for his lover Nadia, and she and Vernon Wise are getting away. Do you know where Tim is?"

Misty kept waving. "I'm so confused. How is Vernon Wise invol—?"

"Where's Tim?" I demanded.

"He and my mom are watching the parade from my apartment building's porch." She motioned toward the Victorian house ahead.

"Kurt, take me to Tim," I said.

Kurt glanced in the rearview mirror. "Misty, sit down."

Holding onto her crown, she slid into the back seat as he hit the gas and zoomed toward her apartment. We waved as he skidded up to the curb and stopped. Misty's mom Eve stood and jogged toward us with a cigarette in her hand.

"Where's Tim?" Misty yelled.

"Detective Harrell just came and picked him up." Eve removed her sunglasses. "There's been a development in Jennifer Coulter's murder investigation."

"Bobbi Sue!" Hemi sprinted toward us. "Are you okay? After you called, I went to find you and saw you dive into the car." Concern flooded his eyes.

"I'm fine, but—" Vernon's truck flew through the intersection. "Vernon's getting away!" I pointed.

"I don't think so." Kurt's muscles tensed. "Mrs. Melchor, call the police and tell them we're in pursuit of Vernon Wise's blue Chevy truck headed west out of Wildcat Springs."

Without a word, Hemi locked eyes with me and leaped over

the door into the passenger's seat—much more gracefully than I had.

Eve dropped her cigarette butt onto the sidewalk. "That's a bad—"

"Buckle up." Kurt tightened his grip on the steering wheel as if he'd been waiting his entire life for this moment.

We fastened our seat belts as Kurt floored it and roared around the corner onto the narrow Walnut Street. I ducked as we thundered by Grandma's house, and I popped up in time to see Kurt nearly sideswipe a station wagon parked on the street. I stifled a gasp as he closed the distance to Vernon's truck. Vernon ran a stop sign, and Misty and I screamed in unison as Kurt blew through it too, narrowly missing a green sedan, whose driver laid on the horn.

Vernon swerved around a corner, and Kurt followed with the Mustang's tires squealing. Vernon was heading out of town, and Shira kept whipping around and shouting at him. Her eyes widened as Kurt drew closer to the vehicle.

Traffic thinned as we sped along a county road lined with corn fields. Sirens wailed, and Kurt looked into the rearview mirror at us. "Sounds like back up's on the way. You ready for me to stop this clown?"

"How?" Hemi asked.

"I'm gonna use my car to strike his truck in the rear corner. Did it to my brother all the time when we were driving go karts."

"No!" Misty and I shrieked in unison.

"I know what I'm doing," Kurt shouted and mashed the accelerator. "Hold on."

Misty clutched my hand, and we screamed as Kurt rammed into the truck, which sent it spinning into the ditch before it came to a rest in the cornfield. Kurt slammed on his brakes while two cars from the sheriff's department roared up behind us and blocked Vernon's path out of the ditch.

"Man, that was an *awesome* move!" Hemi grinned and high-fived Kurt.

Detectives Melchor and Harrell hopped out of their car and raced toward Vernon's truck with their guns drawn.

Shira was shrieking hysterically while Vernon sat with his hands in the air.

"Richard County Sheriff's Department!" Detective Melchor shouted. "Step out of the vehicle with your hands up!"

CHAPTER 25

THAT NIGHT, after Shira and Vernon had been arrested and Misty and I had recovered from our adrenaline rushes, we gathered at Tate's Place. Kurt was reveling in his action hero role and had invited Hemi and Leslie, but they hadn't joined us.

"I don't completely understand everything that happened with Phineas and Vernon," Misty said when we took our seats at the bar. "What's the full story with the jewelry?"

"In May 1934, the Wheeling Brothers Circus stopped in Wildcat Springs," I said. "That's where Phineas met Nadia, the equestrian performer. At the previous stop in Hidden Shores, Indiana, Nadia and her brother had stolen jewelry worth twenty grand. She needed to hide it until it was safe to sell, so she seduced Phineas, and because he worked at the school, he knew about the maintenance tunnel. He loved Nadia, so he hid the jewelry there and waited for her to return."

"But she never came back," Misty said.

"Oh, but she did. She disguised herself, changed her name to Nella Aidan, and got a job teaching at the school. My guess is she intended to retrieve the jewelry without Phineas ever knowing."

"But he figured out what she was doing?" Misty asked.

"Yes. After he'd been waiting all that time, Phineas felt so betrayed and guilty over hiding the stolen jewelry that he hanged himself. After Vernon was hired at the school, he found a suicide note that'd fallen behind Phineas's desk. He'd confessed to hiding the jewelry in the school, but he didn't say where. Vernon kept the secret to himself and searched with the hope that Nadia/Nella hadn't already found the jewelry. Then, earlier this year, when he was diagnosed with lung cancer, he knew his time was running out, so he showed Shira the note and asked for help. She needed money, so she agreed."

"But where does Jennifer fit in?"

"Jennifer was Della Jones-Nash's caretaker, and Della always believed Phineas was murdered. Jennifer wanted to honor Della's memory by finding the truth, but while Jennifer was investigating, she figured out Phineas must've hidden the jewelry for Nadia in the school. Jennifer didn't want anyone to guess that she knew because she really did need the money for herself—"

"Because she had credit card debt from paying for the artificial insemination," Misty added.

"Right. So, Jennifer pretended to be writing a novel to cover her tracks. Eventually, she figured out the hiding place and was on her way back to retrieve the jewelry when Shira killed her. Shira found Leslie's rhinestone and planted it with the hope that the police might suspect her."

Misty sipped her beer. "I told you Flossie Perkins didn't do it."

I laughed. "I have to admit, I'm very happy to be wrong about that one."

The next morning as I was driving to church, I noticed Eduardo Escort's gas gauge was hovering on empty, so I stopped at the station on the edge of Wildcat Springs where I filled the tank and bought a powdered donut for breakfast.

As I was exiting the building, Leslie got out of her Cavalier. I was a little surprised to see her in a Journey concert T-shirt and shorts, but maybe Hemi's church was more casual than mine.

"Morning." I smiled but kept walking toward my car and pinched off a bite of donut.

"I'm leaving," she said. "For good."

I halted and swallowed the donut piece before I choked. "But we cleared your name. Everyone knows Shira Elliot killed Jennifer."

"I know, and I can't thank you enough." She fiddled with a strand of hair. "I . . . I don't belong here, so I've decided to move home. My sister is helping me." She pointed at a skinny blonde who was pumping gas into her Tempo. Now that I was taking a closer look at both of their vehicles, I realized they were packed full of Leslie's belongings.

The breeze ruffled my skirt, and I pushed my sunglasses onto my head as I processed Leslie's news. "What'd Hemi say?"

"He doesn't know. Lorraine and I spent all night packing, and this morning, I told Amanda I wasn't feeling well, so we wouldn't be going to church with them. After she left, we loaded my stuff into our cars."

"You're leaving without even saying good-bye?"

"I left a letter for him."

How thoughtful. "Don't do this to Hemi." I ran my fingers through my hair. "Even if you don't think he's the right man for you, he deserves better than a note. Think about your parents' friendship with Amanda too."

"If I don't leave now, I'll chicken out." She smoothed her hair.

"If you're that uncertain, are you making the right decision? Maybe Hemi would be willing to move to your hometown. Or you could both start over somewhere new. Did you even discuss that with him?"

She stared at her sandals.

I glanced at her ring finger—and her missing engagement ring was all the answer I needed.

"You were right," she finally said. "I can't marry a man I don't love just because my life plan says it's time to get married."

As much as I hurt for Hemi, I couldn't argue with her.

"I need to get going," she said. "Thanks again."

"You're welcome."

While I walked to my car, I reflected that my polite and automatic response didn't feel quite right. Because I certainly didn't welcome the aftermath.

"Do you realize your shenanigans are now causing my *friends* to nearly have heart attacks?" Grandma asked that afternoon as we were eating Sunday dinner at her house.

"Who'd I almost kill this time?" I asked.

"Judy Beeson," she said. "Pass the corn."

I handed her the dish. "And how did I practically induce a myocardial infarction in Judy?"

"Speak plain English. I've told you a thousand times, no one likes a show-off." She dumped a spoonful of overly buttered corn onto her plate next to a half-eaten lump of gluey cheese potatoes. "She witnessed your leap into that Mustang during the parade."

"You're just jealous because you missed the show." The edge of my mouth twitched.

"I don't need the embarrassment of witnessing my granddaughter making a spectacle of herself in front of the entire town."

"That spectacle helped catch a killer." I used a steak knife to saw a piece of pork chop.

"That's why, in spite of my complete and utter humiliation, I'm proud of you."

I set my knife on my plate and looked at my watch. "I'm taking note of the time and date, so I can remember that extremely rare compliment for the rest of my life."

"I'd do the same if I were you." She pointed at my plate, which was, somehow, almost empty. "Save room for dessert."

I had to chew on the dry pork for a while before swallowing. "I should skip it if I'm doomed to be an apple someday."

Grandma waved a hand. "It's Judy Beeson's coconut cream pie. She made me one as a thank you for helping prepare all that food for Tina's family."

I smothered a grin. "Well, in that case—"

"You'd skip dessert if *I* made it?"

"You keep implying I need to watch my figure in order to catch a man."

"You're fine the way you are." Her eyes gleamed. "You just don't like my cooking."

"I like Judy Beeson's pie."

"I don't know what I ever did to deserve such an insensitive granddaughter. I suppose it's your father's influence—oh! Speaking of which . . ." She hopped up and grabbed a small white envelope from the sideboard. "I almost forgot. Someone put this through the mail slot in my front door last night. I found it this morning, and I think it's from your mother." She handed it to me.

The envelope was sealed, and on the front, someone had scrawled *Rochelle & Bobbi Sue*. "It looks like Mom's handwriting," I said. "I'm surprised you didn't open it."

She lifted her chin. "I know my place, young lady."

I withdrew and unfolded the letter that was written on notebook paper in perfect teacher cursive.

Dear Rochelle and Bobbi Sue,

I'm very sorry that your dad and I disappeared without warning. We're safe and will come home as soon as we can. Grandma Spearman will take care of our finances, so don't worry about our bills or next semester's tuition. We love you both and promise that if there had been any other way, we would never have left you.

Love,
Mom and Dad

"Other than the fact that they're safe, this tells me nothing that we didn't already know." I handed the letter to Grandma. "Was there a letter for you?"

"No." She slipped on her glasses and read the letter. "I don't think someone forged your mother's handwriting." She gave the letter back.

I studied the letter. "So, I wonder if Mom and Dad passed through Wildcat Springs last night."

"The same thought crossed my mind."

"If they're still in danger, that seems like a risky move."

She nodded. "If they didn't, they gave the letter to someone they trusted to deliver it."

"And there aren't many people they trust," I said. "They might've given it to Juanita St. James. But I asked her to contact me if she heard from them, so why wouldn't she give it to me personally instead of dropping it in your mail slot?"

"Probably because she knew you'd have too many questions she's not willing—or able—to answer."

"But Rochelle and I need to know where our parents are and what they're doing."

"No, you don't." She sat back in her seat. "Now finish your dinner so we can eat some pie."

After dessert, Grandma and I had called Rochelle at her in-laws' lake house to share the news about Mom and Dad, and though she was happy to hear they were safe, she was as frustrated as I had been by the lack of answers.

On my way home from Grandma's, I'd stopped at a gas station pay phone and called Juanita St. James. I tried her home and work numbers and didn't get an answer at either.

Since I didn't feel comfortable leaving a message, I'd try again tomorrow and—if necessary—the day after that.

When I arrived at home and parked in the driveway, Hemi was getting out of his Bronco. Was he here to blame me for Leslie leaving?

Deciding it was best to play dumb, I stepped out of my car. "Hey, what brings—?"

"Leslie's gone," he said. "She moved home."

"I'm sorry." I clutched my keys, unable to meet his eyes.

"You don't seem surprised."

"I saw her with her sister at the gas station this morning, and she told me."

"I see." He set his jaw.

"How are you holding up?"

"She didn't even have the nerve to dump me in person." He scowled. "I got home from church and found a letter!"

"I pleaded with her to talk to you, but she wouldn't listen."

He narrowed his eyes. "This is your fault."

"How?" I put my hands on my hips. "I did what you asked and proved Leslie didn't kill Jennifer. Leslie should begin her teaching job, marry you next summer, and live happily ever after—all according to your plan."

"You talked her out of our plan."

"She talked herself out of it." I threw my hands in the air. "I'm sorry you're hurting, but if you're madly in love and think you have a future together, go fight for her. Tell her you'll live somewhere you can have a fresh start."

He looked out into the woods. "Is that what you want me to do?"

I stepped closer until he tore his gaze from the trees and looked into my eyes. "If I have any role in this decision whatsoever, we have a very big problem, don't we?"

Chirping birds punctuated the silence until he looked away and said, "I suppose we do." He opened the Bronco's door and stepped behind it. "And I'm sorry. I should be thanking you for helping Leslie instead of blaming you for our problems."

"I did risk my life to find the truth, and riding in a beauty queen's convertible during the parade was no picnic either."

He chuckled. "You've got to stop putting yourself in harm's way, or Duke will be heartbroken."

"Heartbroken is the wrong word to use for a man I'm no longer dating."

"Oh?" he said. "What happened?"

"Grandma Spearman scared him away."

"Huh." There was no mistaking the surprise in his expression. "Your grandma's one of the funniest women I know. She makes me laugh every time she comes into the bookstore," he said. "One day, she even called me an asparagus spear."

Grandma was the only woman I knew who'd say something so outrageous to someone's face. "That didn't offend you?"

"Not at all." He pointed at himself. "I mean, look at me."

I did. "I see more than a vegetable."

He blushed. "So, uh, I'm sorry about Duke. It's his loss."

"That's what I told myself, so it's nice to hear someone else affirm that."

He grinned. "Goodnight, Bobbi Sue. I'll see you around."

"Goodnight."

When I watched him drive away, my stomach issued a flutter that I wanted to ignore but couldn't. It was time to be honest with myself.

Hemi *was* a big deal.

And like it or not, that meant my life might get a little more complicated before I escaped at the end of summer. I smiled as I walked back into the house.

Why had I ever thought Wildcat Springs was boring?

Don't miss Bobbi Sue's next adventure in *The Edge of Knife*. Stay in touch by subscribing to my e-mail newsletter, where you'll get the latest information about my new releases. As a thank you for subscribing, you'll gain access to *Deadly Homestead: A Georgia Rae Winston Mini-Mystery and Other Short Stories*.

If you enjoyed *The Body Electrocution*, I'd be very appreciative if you'd leave a short review to help me spread the word about my novels.

ABOUT THE AUTHOR

Marissa Shrock is a survivor of many awkward blind dates and many years of teaching middle school. Both provide excellent inspiration for her fictional yarns.

Since childhood, she's loved to read a variety of genres, so her own work includes dystopian thrillers and cozy mysteries. She's the author of the Emancipation Warriors Series, the Georgia Rae Winston Mysteries, and the Bobbi Sue Baxter Mysteries. Her debut novel, *The First Principle*, was a Carol Award Finalist.

Marissa enjoys playing golf, building elaborate LEGO creations, and traveling to new places.

Visit her at www.marissashrock.com.

🇬 🅑🅑

ALSO BY MARISSA SHROCK

Georgia Rae Winston Mystery Series

Deadly Harvest

Deadly Holiday

Deadly Heritage

Deadly Harmony

Deadly Hideaway

Deadly Heartbreak

Bobbi Sue Baxter Mysteries

Close Encounters of the Murderous Kind

The Body Electrocution

The Edge of Knife

CREDITS

Editing by A Little Red Ink

Cover Art by Sweet 'N Spicy Designs

Marketing Copy by JR2 Marketing & Advertising

Cimelia Press Logo by Race Point

Beta Readers: Brad and Mary Shrock

www.ingramcontent.com/pod-product-compliance
Lightning Source LLC
Chambersburg PA
CBHW072105170626
46813CB00004B/1469